I0529689

SOME TIME TO LOVE

BY

DAWN SCALA

WOLFCLOUD BOOKS
HARVARD, IL

SOME TIME TO LOVE

ISBN 978-0615791180
Edited by Anton Seda and Dave Mollenkamp
Book Cover design by Wolfcloud Books

Warning Disclaimer

To my husband Anton,
You fill me with inspiration, humor and love,
Love you

SOME TIME TO LOVE

SOME TIME TO LOVE

CONTENTS

SOME TIME TO LOVE

THE MURDER

The girl sat in the dark closet wishing the walls could swallow her up. She knew it wouldn't happen, it never did. Countless times she had made the same wish. Her heart pounding so loud she could hear it. She cringed as something crashed against the wall in the next room. Her mother's faint cries begging him to stop. She could hear her father's slurred voice screaming louder.

"You're nothing but a worthless whore. You are only good for one thing. Now get over here and give me what I want."

Tears streamed down the girls face as she heard her mothers screams. She clamped both of her hands over her ears like she always did. She wished she was big enough to stop her father. One of these days she would. Then her father will be the one who is sorry. For now she would keep her promise to her mother and remain in the closet until she came and got her. A few minutes later, the front door slammed. She breathed a sigh of relief, knowing her father had left. It was the same ritual time after time. She knew her mother would wait a few minutes, making sure her father would not return before coming for her. She heard her mother's footsteps come into the room. She opened the closet door.

"It's okay Becky, you can come out now. He is gone."

The seven year old cautiously crawled out from the back of the closet. She saw her mother's tear streaked face smile at her, as she held out her arms. She quickly ran into them and hugged her back. She let out a gasp.

"I'm sorry Mom," Becky said realizing she was in pain from the beating her father gave her. "Did I hurt you?"

"Oh baby," she cried. "Your hugs could never hurt me." She held her little girl closer. "Now go wash up and I'll make you a sandwich." She wiped the tears from her bruised face. A small trickle of blood oozed from her bottom lip that was beginning to swell.

Becky looked into her mother's tear streaked green eyes. One of them was turning black and blue. Her red hair normally combed neatly, now seemed a mess. Her faded yellow dress that she always wore was torn beyond repair. "I'm scared Mom, why can't we leave? Let's go back to Aunt Molly's and Uncle Ned's. I know Aunt Molly would say yes, please," Becky begged.

She sadly looked down at the floor. "No Becky we can't go there anymore. Ned's tired of taking us in. I'm afraid this time we have to stay here for now. And besides, when you're father gets this bad, he usually stays away for a few days. When he comes home he'll be sorry and sober. You wait and see the worst is over for now."

Mom was right, Becky thought as she boarded the school bus Monday morning. Dad hadn't come home in two days. She took her seat next to Carla like she always did. She listened to what Carla did over the weekend. Becky tried to act interested as Carla recounted how she and her older brother went roller skating with their father. It seemed every week end Carla's father did something with them. Becky secretly envied Carla. When invited over, she noticed how Carla's father would laugh and tease them. Not like her dad, who seemed cold and mean even when sober. Becky never invited Carla over. She was too afraid her dad would come home drunk and embarrass her. She was ashamed of the house they lived in. Carla's house was new and her mom kept a flower garden in back. Becky lived in an old run down farm house that leaked every time it rained.

The next couple of days, Becky went to school and came home and did her homework. Every day she would get off the school bus and carefully sneaked up to the house making sure her dad wasn't there. When she knew the coast was clear, she would run as fast as she could into the house letting the squeaky screen door slam behind her. She headed straight into the kitchen where she would find her mother preparing dinner. She liked it when her dad wasn't there. Her mom seemed happier too, she thought. "What's for dinner," she asked as she set her school books down on the old wooden kitchen table in the middle of the room.

"Chicken," her mom said standing over the counter chopping up vegetables. A car pulled up in the driveway. Becky went to the door to see who it was.

Her eyes grew wide, "it's Dad." She could see the worried look on her mother's face as she quickly looked out the door. They both watched as he staggered out of the car.

"Go to the closet Becky, I'll come and get you later." She watched nervously as her husband approached. "Hurry," she coaxed her away from the door.

Becky ran through the hallway to the bedroom closet and crawled way in the back. She was in total darkness as she listened to the screen door slam. She tightly hugged her knees to her chest and shivered, as her father's voice grew louder.

Ella stood by the counter where she was chopping vegetables. She quickly took the butcher knife she was using and hid it behind her. She made up her mind, if he comes toward me I am going to fight back. She trembled as her sweaty hands gripped the handle of the knife. "Can I fix you something to eat Frank?" She knew there was little food in the house. He had on the same clothes he wore two days before. They were soiled as if he had slept in a nearby dump. His dark brown hair was oily and strands hung down over his face. Ella could smell his stench from across the room. A mixture of body odor and tobacco and alcohol and god knows what else, made her queasy. She suspected she was pregnant, about two months. The anxiety of raising another child with Frank was too much. She wouldn't put another child through what Becky had to live with. She spent endless nights awake worrying about the situation. She felt her world was hopeless. Her friends and family were tired of trying to help her. After years of support, they now gave her the cold treatment. When she called to talk, they would give the excuse they were busy and would call back. But they never did. She felt ashamed. She had no one to turn to, and no place to go.

Frank held on to the nearest kitchen chair for support. "Give me some money," he said with anger. "I know you stash it somewhere."

Ella began to tremble as she saw her husband's bloodshot eyes bearing down on her. "I don't have any Frank, honest."

"You lying bitch." Frank said as he knocked over the chair and began to come toward her. "I guess I'll have to beat it out of you."

Ella gripped the handle of the knife tightly. "I'm warning you Frank, stay away from me." She waited till he was two steps from her before she raised the knife. He grabbed her arm and threw her to the floor. She was no match for him, not even when he was drunk. He got the knife from her and gave her his sick twisted smile before he plunged it deep into her chest.

Frank watched as the blood oozed from his wife's chest. "You dumb bitch, now look what you made me do." He wasn't about to call 911 and wait for the police to take him to jail. No he thought I better get out of here before the kid comes home. He felt remorse thinking his daughter would probably be the one to find her mother. Becky will have to live with the fact that I killed her, he thought. God I need a drink. He stood up and saw her purse on the coffee table in the living room. He quickly walked over to it and turned it upside down. He grabbed the few singles and change that fell to the floor. There was no time to look for more. He walked back into the kitchen and looked down at his wife, before hurrying out the door.

SEVENTEEN YEARS LATER

Melanie's long graceful fingers glided over the piano keys as her sultry green eyes followed the notes on the sheet music. Her heart pounding as she came to the part she always screwed up on. This time she played it through without the mistake. She finished the song feeling proud. She let out a sigh as she began to relax. "Should I play it one more time?" she asked her brother Nathan. He sat on the black leather sofa with his arm resting on the back of the couch. His long blonde hair pulled back in a pony tail. His green eyes sparkling as he spoke.

"It was perfect, now let's go we are running late as it is." He stood up and grabbed his jacket that was next to him. "I don't know why you are so nervous. It's not the first time you've been in a recording studio."

"It's the first time I'll actually be part of the band that is doing the recording. All the other times I was there watching you. This time I'll be on the other side of the glass."

"Melanie, you didn't get into the band because you're my little sister. You're in it because you are good, really good.

Melanie worshipped her older brother Nathan. As far back as she could remember. She followed him everywhere. And for several years he hated it. When he became involved with music at the age of twelve, Nathan begged their parents for a bass guitar for Christmas. Their father was reluctant and said in a few months it would probably end up in the attic. Little did anyone know it would change not only their son's life, but also their daughter's. That bass guitar became part of him. He checked out books from the library and learned notes and some cords. Instead of playing baseball like the other boys in the neighborhood, Nathan would hang out at the music store in town. Nathan began to do odd jobs around the store. In return, Mr. Vanz would give Nathan music lessons. He learned guitar but really loved the sound of the bass. When Melanie became a little older, she would go with Nathan to his lessons and became interested in piano. Soon she was taking lessons and as they grew older, they would often accompany one another. When Melanie was fifteen, Nathan suggested they start their own band. A boy by the name of Todd became their first drummer, and every Saturday afternoon they would practice in the garage. Years later Nathan was asked to join another band. Melanie felt deeply hurt, but understood this new band had paying gigs. It was finally a step up for him. She knew it was time to let go. Even though she was not in the band, she would go to the gigs. Sometimes she would be asked to join in on stage, which was always a thrill. Then the keyboard player Ken was injured in a terrible car accident. He had been drinking too much, and the roads were slippery that night. He lost control of the car and slammed into a tree. His arm was crushed and Doctors were skeptical that he would ever have total use of it again. The band needed another keyboard player and fast. They had gigs coming up and Melanie knew most of the material. Eric Maxwell, who played lead guitar, did not like the idea. He said a chick in a band could only bring trouble. The rest of the guys out voted him, and Melanie was in.

Looking over at the clock on the mantle she saw it was already three thirty. "Shit," she said as she quickly gathered her song sheet and her purse and headed for the door. "We're going to be late again. The guys are going to give us hell." She followed Nathan to his black Camaro and headed toward the expressway that would take them straight into the city and from there to the recording studio. She was thankful traffic wasn't too bad for a Saturday afternoon. Thirty five minutes later, they were running up the stairs. As they walked into the room, everyone became silent. Melanie noticed Eric sitting on the edge of a desk. The rest of the band was standing around him. She saw his disappointed expression right away, and knew he was going to start to yell.

"Did I fail to mention that it costs bookoo bucks to record in this studio?" Eric asked sarcastically as he stubbed out his cigarette.

"I knew it," Melanie said throwing down her sheet music on the table. "You've got a problem with me being in the band. Why don't you just come out with it?"

"Hey," Nathan interrupted. Let's not spend time arguing when we could be recording. The rest of the band agreed and went into the booth and took their positions. Everything was set up and a sound check was done. Eric acknowledged to the soundman Tony they were ready. The drummer Shane, started his drum roll which led into Eric's guitar leads and Nathan's bass. Melanie followed in with her keyboard part and

Eric's clear vocals opened the first chorus, with Nathan joining in on backup. They finished the song and looked toward the soundman in the recording booth.

Tony sat in front of the board contemplating the sound. "That was good, but we need to enhance the chorus." He looked over the board trying to figure out what he could add to make the song sound fuller. He looked at the band in front of him and noticed the pretty woman standing behind the keyboard. "Hey you, what is your name," Tony asked.

"Melanie," she answered as she brushed a strand of her light brown hair with blonde streaks away from her ivory face. She could feel everyone in the band looking at her. "Did I do something wrong?" This is it, she thought. My first time in a studio and this guy knows I'm not good enough. Eric probably paid this guy to throw me out. He's going to ask me to leave, I just know it. Her stomach began to tighten up.

"Can you sing?"

Melanie looked at her brother Nathan for reassurance before answering. She felt relief when she saw his smile. She looked back at the soundman Tony and nodded yes.

"Good, now grab that mike next to you and join in on the chorus." The band started again and Melanie's vocals blended in well. Tony could detect she was nervous but there was no denying it, she was good. Her voice had a unique sound. They recorded a few more songs before it was time for them to quit. "That was great," Tony said as they came out of the room. He lit a cigarette and played back the first song and stopped in the middle. "Now listen to this." He then played the same song but this time with Melanie singing.

"All right," Shane smiled at Melanie as he tapped his foot. "You sound pretty good."

Melanie blushed, "thanks." She felt her face turn a deeper shade of red realizing Eric was watching her. The intensity in his piercing blue eyes made her quiver. She couldn't tell what he was thinking. He showed no emotions whether he liked her voice or not.

"We only need to lay down a couple of more tunes and then we can send the CD's out to agents." Nathan said. "When can we schedule the next recording?"

Tony turned around and grabbed a calendar. "I can pencil you in for Thursday evening next week?"

"That will be fine," Eric said as he glared at Melanie. "It will give us some more rehearsal time with our new vocalist." Eric grabbed his jacket and headed for the door. "See you guys later."

Tony quickly followed Eric out the door. "What is with you?" Tony asked. He knew Eric's moods. Eric had been coming into his studio for years recording his songs. Tony took a liking to the kid and they would spend hours talking about music and jamming together. He liked his style and thought the kid had potential. "Is it the girl? You know she's good. It will be good for your band. She's hot too."

"It is not just the chick." Eric leaned against the wall. "I lost my job. The company was bought out. A lot of people got laid off including me."

"Sorry to hear that." Tony said contemplating an idea he had. "How about working for me? I've been thinking about hiring a manager for my club."

"Are you serious? I don't know anything about being a manger."

"You are smart, I'll teach you. You just have to oversee the rest of the staff, set up the schedule; hire bands that you think will draw a crowd. And not drink all of my profit."

"Would I have to work weekends?"

Tony knew what he was getting at. Eric's band played most weekend evenings. He wouldn't be available to work at the club. "You could be the day manager. Just make sure everything is set up before you leave."

"I don't know man. You really think I can do it?"

"You don't know until you try." Tony smiled at him realizing he really didn't need a manager. But it would free up his time. "Look, meet me at the club tomorrow morning at ten. I have fifteen minutes before the next band comes in, so I have to get back in there. Will I see you tomorrow?"

"Yep, I guess so. Thanks man," Eric shook Tony's hand. "I really appreciate this." Eric took out his keys and headed towards his car.

"Eric can be a real asshole." Nathan said to Shane later that day on the phone. But unless we can replace him and his talent, we'll have to put up with it. Besides, not too many people know the reason why he's like that. I think I'd be an asshole too if I was shuffled around to foster homes."

"Wow man, that had to be hard. What has he told you?"

"He never really talks about it, and I've known him a long time. He has said his parents were drug dealers and addicted themselves. The state came in arrested them and threw Eric into the system. It sounds like his parents were so far gone they had no food and the house was in really bad shape. Eric said he was malnourished when they found him. He was just a kid. I guess they couldn't find any family that would take him in. Going through all those foster care homes could not have been a picnic either," Nathan said. "One night Eric was drunk and told me some things. He said when you are a kid in the foster care program, it is better not to become attached to the family that takes you in. He said it is better that way. Then it does not hurt as much when the state ships you to another home. I think he still believes in that philosophy today. He can be cruel. Like the time we were coming home from that gig and Annette pissed him off."

"The foxy redhead with the wild green eyes," Shane said. "I remember Eric slamming on the brakes and forcing her out of the car in the middle of nowhere. Till this day I have not seen or heard from her. Man, I hope she made it home okay. Eric wouldn't listen to us to turn around. It still shocks me that he did that."

Nathan looked over at his sister sitting in the chair and realized she was listening to the conversation. "I better get going," Nathan didn't want to say anymore in front of her. They set up a time for the next rehearsal and Nathan hung up the phone.

Melanie stood up and grabbed her purse. She smiled at her brother, knowing why he ended the conversation with Shane. Once again he was trying to protect her, she thought. She kissed Nathan on the cheek, "I'm going home. I've got laundry to do."

NIGHTMARES

Becky felt something wet as she wiped her brow and saw the blood on her fingers. As she looked up she saw the blood slowly oozing from the ceiling and the walls. The whole room began to fill with the sticky substance. Drips of blood began to cover her as she searched for a way out of the room. There were no doors, no windows, just walls that were now turning a deep dark color of red. She looked down at her feet and saw her mother, blood seeping from her heart. Her eyes that once sparkled with love every time she spoke to her, were now vacantly staring at her. The wail of her cries woke her up like it always did. She wiped her face feeling the wetness and felt relief to see tears and not blood. It was a sign that the nightmare had ended, for now. She got up and out of bed and walked over to the window and looked out to see only darkness. Like the darkness she felt inside. It happened so many years ago, she was now a young woman, but the nightmares brought it back like it happened yesterday. She remembered having to testify against her father in front of all those people. She felt afraid seeing her father's eyes glare at her as she told everyone in the courtroom what happened to her mother. She was put into the foster care system right away where she stayed with different families over the next three years. She never stayed in one home too long before getting shipped off to another. No one, not even her Aunt Molly and Uncle Ned, would take her in. Although they would come to the court room everyday to watch the trial until it was over. Then she never heard or saw them again. The Canters were the last foster family she was placed with. Becky continued to stare out into the dark recalling her tenth birthday. The day she was hoping to come home from school to find a birthday cake and presents to open. Instead Mrs. Canter seemed upset and told her to go pack her suitcase. She said she no longer could stay with them. A few hours later the social worker came and took her to a group home where there were over fifty children mostly older than she. There were two dorms, one that housed boys and the other for girls. Each dorm had a large room filled with bunk beds. Many of the kids Becky thought seemed disabled either physically or mentally. Often she would go use the washroom and find shit smeared on the walls. The sheets on the beds were old and ripped and mattresses smelled of urine. The older kids would bully the younger ones and the group home workers didn't care if you got beat up or not. No one came to your rescue. There was no one to cry to and tell you everything was going to be okay. No one gave a shit. Becky quickly learned nothing belong to her. Not even the clothes on her back. Any personal items she brought with were stolen. Becky didn't understand why Mrs. Canter sent her away. And why was she here, there was nothing wrong with her. When she asked the social worker she was told it just wasn't a good fit. The group home had very strict rules, and there was limited time allowed to watch television and the food sucked. Then one day it all changed. Becky was outside sitting alone reading a book when she was called into the office and introduced to William Sheldon the third and his wife Carolyn.

"Hello," Carolyn said smiling. "I understand you are twelve years old."

Becky nodded and noticed the lady was holding a doll.

"Carolyn looked down and handed her the doll. "We brought this for you. Do you like it?"

She reached out and took it from her. The doll was stolen from her a few hours later. She had put it down on her bed and after dinner when she returned it was gone. Becky thought she was too old for dolls anyways. After that day there were several more visits from William and Carolyn Sheldon until one day they were there and told her this was the day she would get to go home with them. There was a court date she had to go to and the judge told her from now on William and Carolyn were her parents and her last name was now Sheldon. She lived with them on a huge estate. She was their only child, but Becky didn't mind, in fact she enjoyed it, especially after being with other children at the group home. She had her own room with her own television. She had her own clothes and things and didn't need to worry about anyone taking them. The house had servants so the bathrooms were always clean. The sheets on the bed were changed regularly and smelled good. A few years later she had heard her biological father Frank had died in prison. She didn't know how and Becky didn't care. She was glad he was dead.

TONY

Tony rolled over in bed and grabbed his cell phone that was ringing on his night stand. The caller ID told him it was Eric from his club. "What's up Eric?"

"I caught the son of a bitch last night, Tony. I caught him red handed taking the cash from a customer and stuffing it into his pocket. I had been eyeing him all night. I did like you said, took him out back and made it clear with my fist he was never to step foot near the place again."

"Thanks Eric, you did great. How was the band, did the audience like them?

"I would say so, the crowd stayed till last call. That's always a good sign. After taking out the garbage, I helped Jen behind the bar.   She knew what went down."

"She's the one that tipped you off right?" Tony asked getting out of bed and walking to the kitchen for a cup of coffee.

"Yes she is."

"I'll put in some extra cash with her paycheck. I know she can use it, going to college for any degree isn't cheap. Thanks again Eric, I'll see you Tuesday." Tony hit the button on his cell to disconnect the call.

He poured himself another cup of coffee and sat down on his black leather sofa. He looked out of his living room window that faced the mountains. Every morning he would sit and watch the sun casting shadows over the peaks that nestled around Tahquitz Canyon. He could find peace and tranquility looking at the mountains before his hectic day would start. He was forty-five years old and felt it, not only in his mind but in his body. Being out on the road touring on and off for seven years with his band the "Quick Shots," took its toll. The partying, the drinking, the women, and not getting enough sleep most nights. It was always another town, another gig, another song, trying to keep up with the last hit. Coming up with songs became harder and harder not only for him but for the other guys in the band. By the end of their popularity, they were finding out Ted the drummer was wanted in several states for child support. One night before a gig in Orlando Florida the police walked up to Ted and asked where they could find Ted Sanders. One of the cops showed him an earlier photo of himself, from about five years before when he was heavier and had shorter hair. Ted realized the cops didn't recognize him. He told them "no man, I think they locked him up in some mental institution somewhere. I think it was in New York." He quickly walked away and found Tony. "Sorry man, you got to do this gig without me, I'm out of here." Tony made some quick phone calls and they were able to find another drummer for the night. But Ted was a phenomenal on drums and the band really didn't want to lose him. Ted started to wear a disguise to most concerts and was given another name when Tony announced the players. Mike O'day their agent was informed and often called Ted to ask "Are you up to date on your child support in Wyoming?" Or whatever state it was. "We have a gig coming up there."

The music was changing, or maybe they were getting older. The concerts weren't selling out anymore. CD sales were dropping. He had been thinking of buying a club for years. He had been introduced to a local realtor Bill, at a party he attended one evening. After a few months of looking at buildings in the Palm Springs area he found a nice size place that was once a warehouse for clothing right outside of town. It was the time to settle down in one place. He liked California. Weather was decent with its beautiful mountains and palm trees. Most of the guys in the band over the years had married and had kids and had decided to make California their home. Most marriages didn't work out. The wives found it hard to have their husbands on the road. And the guys usually would get lonely and screw the first chick that came onto them. Eventually all hell would break loose. Tony knew early on that having a family and being on the road would not be for him. From time to time his mind would remember Connie. She was a tall beautiful brunette and smart and everything he thought he could want in a woman. He had fallen hard for her. Than the night the band got offered a signed contract with a label, Connie found out she was pregnant. That was the end of that. He took off on the road with the band and as far he knew, she had an abortion like they discussed before he left. He never heard from her again. He soon learned being a good looking guitar player in a hot rock and roll band had benefits. Tony smiled remembering there was never a shortage of good looking woman that would have sex with him. Sometimes he would have more than one woman a night. Depending where his energy level was and how much he had to drink. That was his thing, drinking and women. He never got into the drug scene.

There were too many good musicians that went down that road and for most of them, never came back. It was also his rule once they signed the recording contract, no drugs in the band or you were out. But for the lack of drug use, they made up in alcohol.

Tony sat on his sofa with his coffee in his hand looking at his collection of photos taken over the years of famous musicians he played with and band members and friends. He felt sadness creep in as he knew none of the photos were of family.

The phone interrupted his thoughts. He always looked at the caller ID that would determine if he was going to answer it or let it go to voice mail. He was surprised when he saw the name.

"Alex, wow how have you been?" Tony asked not remembering when the last time he had spoken to his old bass player from the Quick Shots.

"Hey Tony, it's good to hear your voice. But I'm afraid I'm calling with some bad news. I just got a call from Mike O'Day. He said Ted died last night."

"How," he asked as images of Ted pounding his drums with his sticks and his quirky smile that always got him laid flashed into Tony's mind.

"They think it was a heart attack. He complained after the gig he was playing that he didn't feel good and his upper arm was hurting. They were loading equipment and this chick, I think her name is Wanda, said he grabbed his chest and fell to the floor. The owner called 911 but by the time they got there it was too late. He was gone that fast. They will know more when they do the autopsy. Shit Tony, he was only forty five."

Tony's eyes began to tear. "He always did like to party. He was like a brother to me. I can't believe he's gone."

"Yeah me too, their thinking of having him buried back home in Illinois."

"Have you gotten a hold of anyone else?" Tony was thinking of his other band buddies from the Quick Shots.

"You were the first person I've called so far. Look, can you call Danny? And I'll call Steve. I want to tell them before the press gets a hold of this."

"Yeah, the press is going to have a field day with this, another rock and roll idol gone. At least they can't blame this one on drugs."

"Ted did way too much drinking. He never would slow down when it came to that."

Tony chuckled, "or the women. How many kids does he have?"

"I don't think anyone really knows. I told him to wear rubbers man," Alex said.

"That wasn't his style."

"I'll give you a call when I know more. Maybe we can all catch the same flight to Illinois and reminisce on old times."

"That sounds good Alex. It won't be the same without Ted though."

"I know," Alex said holding back the tears. "I'll call you later."

Tony hung up feeling the tears roll down his face. He remembered the last time with Ted. Even as he got older, he still had his good looks and brash behavior which women seemed to love. A few times a year he would come into his club and sit at a table surrounded by beautiful women. Ted would later give him that smile saying "I still got it man, still got it." Tony would laugh and say back, "yeah Ted you still got it, but be careful on what you might get."

SECOND THOUGHTS

Eric stopped at the local coffee shop in town for dinner before heading up to the mountains. He had finished the day at Tony's club. Things were going pretty good and he was enjoying himself. He had listened to two bands on CD and called to book them for the following month. No one gave him any hassle and he got along with everyone he worked with. Tony had set up an office for him in the back of the club across from his office. The staff seemed to respect Tony's decision on hiring him as the manager. They came to him with questions and if he didn't know the answer they would suggest what Tony might do in that situation. Or he would call Tony himself. He wanted to keep the man happy.

The waitress waived to him as he seated himself at a nearby table. She quickly came over with her pen and pad ready to take his order.

"I'll have the cheeseburger deluxe and..." Eric's words trailed off as he noticed the customer walking in the door. His first reaction was he did not want to be seen. A hesitant smile came over her face as she walked slowly towards him. Realizing the waitress was still waiting for his order he replied, "and coffee." The waitress had walked off and Melanie was now standing beside him.

"Have a seat." Eric said to her as he noticed how uncomfortable she seemed.

"I just came over to say hi, I don't want to bother you."

Eric remembered what a jerk he had been to her in the studio. "No sit down, please," he added noticing she still hesitated.

"I was on my way home from work and thought I would get a bite to eat." Melanie replied as she sat down in the booth across from Eric. The waitress returned to pour coffee for Eric and Melanie turned over her cup indicating she would also have some.

"Would you like anything else?" The waitress asked.

"I'll have the turkey club on wheat." She said turning her attention back to Eric. So, do you eat here often?"

"I usually come here before I go up to the Tahquitz Canyon."

"I haven't been there for a few years. You can get so caught up in everyday life you forget how beautiful these mountains are." Melanie's green eyes turned toward the window to look out.

"Your brother Nathan is a good bass player. He seems to grasp my ideas I want in my songs."

Melanie returned her gaze to Eric. "Thank you, I'll let him know you think so, and what about me? Do you think I'll be able to grasp your ideas?"

"It is too soon to tell." Eric said eyeing her sternly. "I'll have you know, I'm not fond of having females in my band."

"I can tell. And why is that Eric?" Melanie asked in a defensive manor.

The waitress appeared with their food. He watched Melanie as she tossed her long wavy brown hair with blonde steaks away from her face before taking a bite from her sandwich. She looked up with her green eyes returning to his waiting for an answer. Eric ignored her question and began to eat. A minute of silence passed between the two before his cell phone rang. "Hey Tony," Eric answered as he looked at Melanie letting her know who it was he was speaking to.

"Hi Eric, look I have to go out of town this week. My drummer died, and the funeral is going to be in Woodstock Illinois. I need to know can you handle the club while I'm away? And I'm wondering if you want to reschedule the recording or would you be okay if I had someone else come in and do it?"

"Wow, sorry to hear that. Don't worry about the club." Eric remembered hearing stories and seeing photos in Tony's studio about the drummer from the Quick Shots. "He was a wild cat on drums, what happened?"

"Heart attack, are you okay with re scheduling. I have other bands to call also."

Eric could hear the stress in Tony's voice. "Who is this guy that would be recording us? You know what, never mind. We will wait till you are ready. I like what you do with our sound and I'm in no hurry. Don't worry about the club, and I will keep in touch with you. Again, I'm sorry to hear about your friend."

"Thanks man," Tony said relieved. "I'll talk to you later."

Eric put his phone on the table and turned his attention to Melanie. "It looks like we will have more time to rehearse. Tony's drummer died of a heart attack. He is going to Illinois for the funeral. I imagine recording time will be put off for a while."

Eric's eyes turned to the mountains outside the window. "You feel like taking a ride with me up to Tahquitz Canyon?"

Surprise came over Melanie's face. "Sure," she answered wiping her mouth with a napkin.

They finished their meal and Eric paid for Melanie's. "We'll take my car," he said. He saw her hesitate. He grinned "Don't worry, I don't bite."

"That's not what I heard. And you should smile more, it looks good on you." Melanie followed Eric to his white Chevy across the street and got in on the passenger side. Eric started his car and drove up Mesquite road pulling into the parking lot. There was only one other car. Eric took out his backpack that he always brought with him on the trail. He grabbed an extra water bottle for Melanie and sunglasses.

"I like coming here during the week when it's not crowded," Eric said looking down at her feet. "Can you hike in those?"

"Melanie was wearing a light blue dress and sandals. "We will find out." She answered pulling out a black band out of her purse to hold back her hair that was blowing in the wind. "Lead the way."

The day was warm and the sun showed the canyon's beautiful red and brown desert rock formation along the ridges high above them as they walked along the trail leading to the sixty foot waterfall. They still had a few hours left before the canyon closed.

"I can't believe how beautiful this is," Melanie stopped to take a break sitting down on a rock.

Eric handed her a bottle of water and pulled another one out for him. "It is incredible. Look over there," pointing to the eagle flying above them. "Come on, were almost there." Eric extended his hand to Melanie helping her up. Ten minutes later they could see and hear the steady rush of water falling sixty feet to the ground. "We can sit over there." Eric grabbed Melanie's hand.

"Wait," she said noting she would be walking on rocks to cross the creek. "I'm less likely to fall in my bare feet." She slipped off her sandals.

Eric took them from her and put the shoes inside his backpack. He then took her hand and led her over the trail of standing rocks in the creek stopping right in front of the water fall. The mist of the water splashing down on them felt cool and refreshing. "I could stay here forever and just write songs." He said looking up at the top of the rocks watching the water pour down from the upper mountains.

"Is that why you come here, to write songs?"

Eric looked down at her and noticed how beautiful she looked with strands of her brown hair blowing across her white skin and her green eyes that held a hint of innocence and curiosity to the question she had asked. Without even thinking, he took her into his arms and kissed her soft lips. He felt himself getting excited as she leaned her body into his. He wanted to take her right then and there. He wanted to feel himself deep within her. What was he thinking? Eric pushed Melanie away. "I have to go," he said roughly. "It is getting late."

Melanie gave him a startled look. "Okay, did I do something wrong?"

"Look," he said coldly. "It's just not a good idea, do you understand?" His voice became louder. "I don't need complications in my life. If you want to remain in my band I suggest you keep your distance."

Melanie's face went from being startled to angry. "You won't have to worry about that." She turned abruptly away and started walking the way they came in. She stopped suddenly, "can I have my shoes back please?"

Eric reached in his backpack and handed them to her and watched as she slipped them on. It was a long silent walk back to his car. The sun was now descending over the mountains. He felt a chill in the air and knew it was meant for him. He had wished they had taken separate cars. "Look Melanie," he said before opening the car door for her. "I am sorry for being such an ass. I didn't mean to shove you away like that. I just don't think it would be a good idea for us to get involved and be in the same band. Can you understand where I'm coming from?

Melanie stood there for a moment watching him before answering. "I agree, your right," as she pushed her hair away from her face. "It would be better if we remain neutral towards one another."

He opened the car door for her feeling relieved. "I'm glad you see it the same way." He got in and started the car. "Don't forget we have the gig next Friday night. And Sunday, I was hoping we could get together and go over some new songs I wrote. Is Sunday good for you and your brother?"

Melanie was looking out the side window watching the sun set. "I'll give him a call. I'm sure it will be fine."

Eric pulled up to where she parked her car. "Great, I'll give you a call when I find out what day works out with the rest of the band." Melanie opened the car door and stepped out.

"Thanks Eric for the meal. I'll talk to you soon." She closed the door and walked over to her car.

Eric made sure she got in before pulling away. He would have to keep his head level and distant himself from that one. It had been a few weeks since he had gotten laid. It was time to pay Becky a visit. He pulled out his cell phone and called her at the next stop light. "Hey what are you doing," he asked upon hearing her familiar voice.

"Mmm Eric, I was just about to curl up on the couch with a good movie. Care to join me?"

Eric grinned knowing it would be an open invitation. "I'll stop and get your favorite bottle of wine. Do you need anything else?"

"Just you baby." Becky purred into the phone.

"What is the movie?"

"Does it matter?"

Eric smiled, still having an erection from kissing Melanie. "I'm on my way."

"Hurry baby, don't keep me waiting."

Eric arrived at her apartment about twenty minutes later. He followed her into the kitchen as she retrieved two wine glasses from her cupboard. Her bleached blonde hair hanging down over her sheer black nightgown with matching black lace underwear excited him as always. Her makeup looked as if she just put it on and she smelled of a lightly scented perfume. He came up behind her and grabbed her breasts and began kissing her neck. "You smell so good." His hands pulling down the flimsy lace underwear reaching down between her legs, she began to moan. He turned her around and lifted her onto the counter. She removed the top of her nightgown and eagerly spread her legs as he began kissing her mouth, her breasts and down to the spot he loved the most. When her moans became louder Eric carried her to the bed and laid her down and quickly removed his clothes. He stood before her naked as she took him into her mouth while stroking him. He was ready to explode and could not stand it any longer. Gently pulling away he mounted her holding back until he felt she was ready to come, he then quickened his thrusts. Her nails digging into his back and then releasing as her body began to relax.

"Shit," Eric yelled rolling off of her. "You have to cut those things. You are leaving me scars."

"Oh baby, I'm just marking my territory." Becky said rolling on her stomach to face him. "I'm sorry do you forgive me? She smiled kissing his lips.

"I'm not your territory." He knew he should quit having sex with her. She wanted a relationship with him and he had been honest from the start, when he told her that wasn't his intentions. She wasn't taking no for an answer. One night when they were both pretty drunk, Eric made the mistake and told Becky about his parents and being raised in the foster care system. To his surprise she said she also was placed in foster care until her adoption. He remembered the strange smile Becky gave him saying they were meant to be together. After that night she would come to the gigs in short dresses and high boots with her boobs hanging out and come up to him after the show rubbing herself up against him. She made it too easy for him. Her actions also chased away any other woman he might have had his eye on that evening. If he were talking to any woman, Becky would quickly run up beside him and slip her arm around his waist. He was getting fed up with her behavior and knew it was his fault for always giving in.

"Where is your next show?" Becky asked running her fingers up and down his chest.

"I don't know. I have to look at the schedule." He pretended not to know. It did not matter. She would look at his bands website online and find out where they were playing. He rolled out of bed and began to dress. Feeling irritated for coming over.

Becky's face began to pout. "Are you leaving baby? We didn't have our wine yet?"

"I have a lot to do tomorrow," he lied. "I need to get some sleep."

"You can sleep here," Becky said grabbing his hand trying to stop him from pulling up his pants.

Eric grinned, "I know if I stay neither one of us will get any sleep." He finished getting dressed and headed for the door.

"Call me." Becky said giving Eric a kiss on the lips.

Eric nodded knowing he had no intentions of calling her. He needed to cool things with her no matter how horny he got. His thoughts returned to Melanie as he drove home.

RETURNING TO ILLINOIS

Tony finished going through the security check at the Palm Springs International airport. He grabbed his carry-on luggage and his wallet, keys, phone out of the tray when he heard a familiar voice calling his name. Slipping on his shoes he turned to see Alex coming towards him.

"Hey Tony," Alex greeted him with a hug. "Good to see you. I'm glad we were able to take the same flight on short notice."

"Yeah, me too, do you know if Danny and Steve are here yet?"

Alex shook his head. "I have not seen Steve and Danny's in the washroom getting sick. He hates flying man."

Tony laughed. "Do you remember the hell we had trying to get him on the plane when we had to tour Europe? I thought for sure I was going to have to play guitar." Tony was not only the singer but had played some guitar when the band first started. Tony didn't like the idea of having someone else play the lead. But when he heard Danny play their songs throwing rifts in that Tony could not duplicate, he knew Danny would be right for the band. "How did we get him on the plane?"

"Steve slipped him some kind of downer in his drink."

"Yeah, now I remember, boy was he pissed when he found out."

"You sons of bitches better not try anything like that again." Danny said walking up behind them.

"But it worked man, you slept almost the entire flight. In fact we were worried you were going to get us kicked off the plane because of your snoring."

"Hey Danny," Tony slapped him on the back. "How are you feeling? It looks like you've put on some weight since I've seen you last." Danny's black hair was now showing signs of grey. He was taller than him and had always been a good looking guy, but too skinny, Tony thought. He had suspected Danny was into cocaine at the time they were touring but could never prove it. He had asked the other guys about it but no one would say. Tony was totally against drugs and they all knew it.

"Yeah I'll be okay. This whole thing with Ted has me freaked out you know. I can't believe he is gone."

They announced boarding for Milwaukee and Tony saw Steve running towards them. "Hey," Tony said, "I wasn't sure if you were going to make it?"

"The old lady is giving me shit." Steve said catching his breath. "I have a mind just to stay in Illinois and not come home."

"What is she bitchin about now?" Alex asked.

"Shit, I don't know, she thinks I'm cheating on her." Steve said in frustration.

"Are you?" Tony asked smiling knowing the answer.

"Well, yeah, but there is no way she could possible know for sure, I don't think."

They boarded the plane and put their luggage in the overhead compartments and took their seats. Tony was seated next to Steve and Danny and Alex sat across the aisle from them. It was an easy take off and once in the sky Tony noticed Danny seemed more at ease. Alex took out a book and began to read.

Steve took out his comb and ran it through his dark brown hair. He had inherited his good looks from his mother's side which came over from Italy. She had taught him the language and he used it when romancing women.

"You've been married to Patti, what two years now? And you are cheating on her already?" Tony asked.

"Things were cool at first. Everything was great. Then she said she wanted a baby. That's all she talks about. She won't leave me alone about it. I'm passed that. I already have five from my other two marriages. And they are almost all grown. I don't want another kid. I've been hanging out at Nellie's bar and the owner, Nellie; well let's just say we've been getting along really good." A sly smile came over Steve's face.

Tony shook his head. "What were you thinking man, marrying a twenty-five year old? Of course she is going to want kids. I can't believe you didn't have this conversation with her before marrying her."

"Listen to you, old wise one. Didn't you get some chick knocked up years ago?"

Tony sighed, "yes but I made it clear to her I wasn't ready for kids or marriage and she had an abortion. And that was that, the band took off on tour and I never heard from her again."

"Do you ever regret not having kids?" Steve asked.

"My life is what I chose it to be." Tony closed his eyes, his memories going back twenty-four years. It was the evening after he found out his band "The Quick Shots" were getting a signed deal with a major label. He was hung over and hadn't slept. He had gone over to Connie's the next evening to share the exciting news.

He was expecting a warm welcome. Following her into the living room and sitting next to her on the sofa. He tried to apologize for not calling her sooner. "We were up all night celebrating," he had told her. "Mike O'Day wants us sign a contract with "Tri Recording". He went on talking about how they needed to find an agent and would start touring.

Connie with her black hair and crystal blue eyes sat silent for a moment. "I was up all last night, too. You should have called, Tony. You haven't asked me once how I am. You've been going on and on about the band. Did you forget last night I passed out on the dance floor?" She began to cry. "I'm pregnant."

Little did he realize his next words would haunt him. Telling her, "this is not a good time Connie. I'm going on the road. I won't be around to be a daddy. I'm not ready to settle down and have a family. Having an abortion was the only way to go." Memories of her tears streaking down her beautiful face, knowing he had broken her heart.

Reporters rushed up to them with their microphones and cameras as they entered the terminal. "How did Ted really die?" "Was it an overdose?" Ted's death had hit the celebrity news channels showing old photos of him and the band. Tony had almost forgotten how it was to be bombarded by the press. In Palm Springs people would recognize him and just nod. The press was now drawing attention from other people who would stop and look.

"Come on guys," Steve said to the reporters. "Let us through."

Alex who always enjoyed the press spoke up. "We all loved Ted and we will miss him very much."

It was like bait to fish when Alex spoke up. The reporters surrounded him with their microphones asking more questions. "How long will you be staying in the Midwest?" "Is there a chance this will bring you back together for another CD?" The press followed them outside where a limo was waiting. Tony was glad he had brought his black leather jacket. Gray skies and chilly temperatures for the next week were in the forecast.

"This weather sucks man. I already want to go home." Danny said once they were all seated in the limo. "Does anyone know where we are staying?"

"The Holiday Inn in Crystal Lake, it's not far from Woodstock where the funeral will be," Alex replied.

Tony's parents had passed away years ago and he never stayed in touch with anyone from his home town. Once the band took off, his life changed. He no longer felt like the same person. It was all about the band, the audience and the music. It consumed every waking minute. It was never ending parties, drinking, and women. And then there was the stress of having to get to the next gig. Their audiences were getting bigger, and they were selling out concerts. He loved all of it. There was no reason for him to come back. He wondered if Connie still lived in the area. Probably married and has five kids now. He had tried years ago to look her up on the internet with no success. It was probably not a good idea. He had been such an asshole to her. He had left her to get an abortion. Not even talking to her afterwards to see how she was doing. They arrived at the hotel a couple of hours later. They booked separate rooms. Something the band had always done. They never wanted to infringe on each other's privacy. After checking in, they agreed to meet in the hotel's restaurant at seven.   Tony went to his room and unpacked.

MELANIE

Melanie looked at the clock on the wall across from her desk and thought the day would never end. She had been looking forward to this evening. They were playing at a decent club outside of town and she had gone there a few times to listen to other bands. But this evening she would be playing. She needed to go straight home after work and get ready. Load in was at eight PM and it was almost five.

"So we finally get to hear you play, Melanie. What time do you want us there?"

Melanie smiled at her co-workers Dale and Ann who were walking towards her. She quickly gathered her notes from the day's events of clients who called wanting travel information. She enjoyed her job and was good at it. Being a travel agent had its perks. She would get discounts on her own trips. Two years ago she had gone to the Bahamas with her then boyfriend Perry who played guitar.

"We go on at nine." Melanie turned off her computer and stood up grabbing her keys out of her purse and followed Dale and Ann out with Dale locking the door behind them. "Just a word of advice, don't sit too close to the stage. One, the band will be loud and two, there is almost always somebody falling down drunk on the dance floor.

"Good to know," Ann said as she looked at Dale.

Melanie smiled. She enjoyed working for them. And thought they made a perfect couple. They were in their mid thirties with two children. They had a boy and a girl. They had hired her four years ago for their travel agency. Taking a chance on her with no experience she was very grateful. Over the years Ann had taken her under her wing teaching her the business. "I'll see you there tonight." Melanie hurried towards her car waving good-bye. She got home and heated up some left over spaghetti and quickly put the dishes in the dishwasher. She then walked into her bedroom stripping off her work clothes and getting into the shower. Letting the warm water run over her head as she washed her hair and shaved her long legs. Grabbing a towel she dried herself off and went to her closet to pick out her favorite mini green dress with thin straps that accented her green eyes and showed off her long tan legs. She put on a gold necklace with a round medallion design that she had bought a couple of weeks ago in one of the shops, downtown Palm Springs. She applied her make-up, adding extra black eyeliner to accent her eyes and pink lipstick. She then took her curling iron to her different layers of her soft highlighted hair to add volume. Satisfied with her looks, she sprayed her favorite perfume on. She slipped on her flat shoes and put her high heeled sandals into her bag. She would change into them before the show. Grabbing her keyboard carrying case she went out to her car and put it into her trunk and returned with her stand and microphone. Twenty minutes later she arrived at the club seeing Eric and her brother unloading the trailer. She casually stepped out of her car and grabbed her things along with her keyboard case and walked over to them. "How is it going guys?"

Eric turned to look at Melanie. "Good," he said eyeing her up and down. "I'll show you where we are setting up." He grabbed the PA and led the way into the club. Nathan grabbed some gear and followed behind Melanie. They walked past the tables and bar that would soon be filled with people to a stage where the drummer Shane was setting up.

"Hi Melanie," Shane said looking up from his stand.

"Hello," Melanie smiled turning back to Eric. "Where do you want me?"

"I'll be here." Eric stood in the middle of the stage. "Your brother will be next to me. We will put your keys off to the side. Is that okay with you?"

Melanie stood facing the stage. "That should be fine." She laid down her gear and went out to her car to get the remainder of her stuff. She proceeded to help load in the items that was not too heavy like wires and stands. After going to the washroom too comb her hair and change her shoes, she went to the bar and ordered a Long Island ice tea. The place was starting to get crowded when she noticed Dale and Ann just coming in. "You better grab a table now if you want to sit." The bartender brought her drink and she joined them near a booth close to the stage. She stood there taking a sip when Eric signaled her to come to the stage. "Got to go," she said to Ann and Dale, "the boss is calling me." She turned and walked toward Eric.

"This is the song list we will be doing." Eric handed her a sheet of paper.

Melanie looked over the sheet and nodded her head while taking a sip of her drink. "Where do you want me to come in on this song?"

"Hey baby," Becky said walking up to Eric holding a drink in one hand while slipping her other arm around his waist. "Did you get home okay the other night?"

Melanie noticed Eric's face turned to disgust as he took her arm away from him causing her to spill some of her drink. "Why don't you go and sit down. We have to finish setting up."

"Okay baby, you are always so grumpy before a gig." She turned toward Melanie and glared at her before walking away and sitting at a table close to the stage.

"Who is that?" Melanie asked Eric as she watched the woman walk away wearing a pair of black high stilettos shoes and tight blue jeans.

"That is Becky." Nathan whispered into Melanie's ear walking onto the stage.

"She's a pain in the ass, is what she is." Eric replied. "What were you asking me before? Oh, yes, I remember now. I'll signal you when to come in."

They finished plugging in cords for the microphones and her keyboard. Shane was now sitting behind his DW kit kicking the base drum for sound. Eric went to the bar and ordered a White Russian returning to the stage picked up his guitar strummed a few cords and did some adjustments on the sound board. He then turned to the rest of the band. "Are we ready?" When everyone said yes, Eric turned to the microphone. "Hello, I want to thank everyone for coming out tonight. We are "The Fifth Degree." Shane counted, "one, two, three, and the band started on four. It was one of the originals that Eric had written. The second song people started dancing.

Melanie kept her eye on Eric and watched for his ques. When he nodded, she would join him on harmony singing. More people were coming into the club and every table was filled. People stood wall to wall watching them and applauding after every song. Eric would signal when he wanted someone to do a solo. The rest of the band except for the drummer would stop. Melanie let loose on her keys when it came her turn. She was overwhelmed by the audience response. They clapped and whistled more for her than anyone else in the band. Nathan looked over at her and smiled proudly, but she couldn't tell if Eric was pleased. He then went into his solo stepping off the stage into the crowd while playing his wireless guitar. Becky, who seemed quite drunk, was dancing by herself and quickly went up to Eric grinding her hips back and forth with her arms above her head. Eric continued playing and stepped back on stage looking over to Melanie as if to see what her reaction was.

"We are going to take a short break so don't go away." Eric said into the microphone. He put his guitar down and headed towards the bar.

Melanie noticed Becky was quick to follow him. "Is she Eric's girlfriend?"

Nathan stepped off the stage and laughed. "No, but she thinks she is. He just hooks up with her when he is horny."

Melanie wanted another drink and the only opening in the bar was where Eric and Becky were standing. "Long Island ice tea," she told the bartender standing behind Eric.

"And you," Becky slurred loudly. "Why the fuck do you keep staring at Eric? I bet you think your hot shit because you sing and play piano. Well honey, you sound like shit and...."

Eric quickly grabbed Becky's arm and pulled her away from the bar. "Shut the fuck up," he said in a low voice. "You need to go home."

Becky's red eyes glared back at Melanie. "Who did you fuck to get into the band?" She yelled.

People that were standing close were watching the scene. Melanie's anger quickly rose. "Go home and sleep it off you bitch."

Becky eyes widened and took a step toward Melanie. Eric's grip tightened around her arm and forced her towards the door. "Leave and I don't want you coming to any more of my shows."

"Oh baby, I'm sorry, I'll be a good girl I promise."

He had gotten her outside the building now where no one could hear her. She turned to try and kiss him but he pushed her away. "Look, I'm done with you."

Becky stumbled while trying to find her car keys in her purse. Tears were now streaking down her face. "You'll come back to me. You always do," she said as she walked away.

"Break is over." Nathan said standing next to Eric watching Becky get into her car.

"Yep, break is over." Eric turned and walked back into the building. "I'm really sorry about that," he said to Melanie as they were getting ready to play.

Melanie shrugged her shoulders, "its okay, and no big deal."

"I'm disappointed." Shane said with a smile as he grabbed his sticks. "I was hoping for a cat fight."

Nathan laughed as he adjusted his strap to his bass. "Yeah, well Melanie would have won. I'm telling you she was always beating me up when I was little."

"And it's a shame I still can." Melanie joked back. "You were always a pussy."

They all laughed and broke into a song. The rest of the evening went smoothly. The incident somehow made Melanie feel more at ease with Eric and Shane. It felt like she had broken the ice. She could handle herself and now they knew it. She noticed the guy standing at the bar kept smiling at her when she looked at him. He was tall and very good looking in a rugged sort of way. He had high cheek bones with dark hair and a sharp chin with a goatee. He was dressed in a black t-shirt with a picture of a white wolf and jeans. Melanie was hoping he would stick around after the show.

"I want to thank everyone for coming out to see us tonight." Eric said to the crowd after finishing the last song. "Hope you had a good time and don't forget to check out our website to see where we will be next." The crowd applauded and Melanie unplugged her microphone and her keyboard and started wrapping her cords.

"Can I buy you a drink?"

Melanie looked up to see the handsome guy she had been watching standing in front of her. "Sure," she said as she stepped down from the stage throwing the cords into her bag. "I'll have a Long Island Ice Tea." She followed him over to the bar.

"I thought the show was good and I'm not just talking about the one on stage," he said as he ordered her drink. "My name is Trent. I've seen your band play here before but don't remember you."

"I'm Melanie," taking a sip of her drink as she leaned against the bar. "I'm replacing Ken the other keyboard player. He was in a bad car accident and screwed up his arm. They don't think he'll be able to play again."

"Wow that is too bad. So how do you know these guys?"

"Nathan is my brother." Melanie pointed over to him who was busy packing up the equipment.

"Do you mind helping us here? I want to go home." Eric yelled to her as he was unplugging cords from the PA.

"I better help tear down or knowing him he will find another keyboard player." Melanie started to walk away when Trent grabbed her arm lightly.

"It's early, would you like to go have a drink? I know another place that is open till four."

Melanie felt an electrical charge when Trent touched her. His eyes held a glint of desire for her. She looked over at Eric who was still watching her. He gave her a dismal look and seemed frustrated by her actions. Why should it bother him? She thought. He had his own little show going on earlier with Becky. He probably wanted the band to pack up in a hurry so he could go screw her. "Yeah, why not," she said turning to Trent with a half smile. "Let me finish up here."

Thirty minutes later the truck was loaded and Eric turned to her. "Do you know that guy?" Nodding toward Trent, who was standing near the door.

"Not really, do you? We are just going to get a drink. Do you want to come?" Melanie took out her keys from her purse. Part of her wanting him to say yes and part of her hoping he would say no.

"I'll pass," Eric said handing her a hundred dollar bill for the gig. Eric's phone began to ring. He reached into his pocket and looked at the caller ID. "What the fuck, she's called me five times and has left me four texts since she left here."

"Who do you mean, Becky?" Nathan asked standing beside Eric.

"What's going on?" Shane asked joining his band mates.

"What does she say? Is she still threatening to kick my ass?" Melanie asked.

Eric put his phone on speaker so everyone could hear and played his voice mail. Becky's voice was almost a growl, "I know you are fucking her. How dare you do this to me, I hate you." Eric played the next message. You could hear her sniffles and her voice pleading. "I'm so sorry I said that. Please forgive me Eric. I really do love you, call me."

"She is one jealous bitch." Melanie said.

"You mean crazy." Eric scrolled through some of the texts and read them out loud. "Please come over I am sitting here wearing my black laced panties getting excited thinking about you." Just then his phone rang again. Eric looked at the caller ID and shook his head and answered it. "I want you to leave me the fuck alone. Don't call me anymore, don't text me anymore and don't come to my shows. I won't have anything more to do with you, understood?" Eric ended the call. A second later it rang again.

"Wow she is beyond crazy." Shane said. "Put her number on silent."

"How do I do that?" Eric asked.

"Here give me your phone." Shane took Eric's phone and did the adjustment. "Now when she calls you, the phone won't ring. But it will go to voicemail. You can also call your carrier and I think they can block her calls and texts."

"Thanks," Eric said taking his phone back.

Nathan turned to Melanie and hugged and kissed her. "Love you sis. Are you okay to drive?"

"She has company." Eric replied.

"I'll be fine, the night is young and I feel like dancing. I'll call you tomorrow." She kissed her brother and waved to Eric and Shane as she walked toward Trent. Was that genuine concern Eric showed for her when he asked if she knew him? Maybe he wasn't as cold hearted as he led everyone to believe. It didn't matter she had no intentions of getting involved in his little soap opera drama. She wanted to take her own car and follow Trent. This way if she felt like leaving she could. The place was a smaller club outside of town. The parking lot was half filled and loud music could be heard from outside. There was a fee to get in and Trent insisted he pay for her. Once inside they found a quaint little booth in the back with a candle on the table. Trent sat next to her and ordered her a drink and a beer for himself.

"The band here is pretty decent don't you think?" Melanie said noticing the members who were probably in their forties.

"Not as good as your band." Smiling, Trent stood up and took her hand. "Come on let's dance." Trent led her to an open spot and put one arm around her waist taking a few steps away from her and twirling her in a circle.

"Wow you are good." Melanie laughed following his lead.

"I live to dance." Trent said as he twirled Melanie again.

"You weren't dancing when I was playing."

"I wanted my first dance of the evening to be with you."

"Yeah right," she laughed. Melanie didn't believe that line but felt flattered. They continued dancing to the next two songs and then sitting down and ordering two more drinks. Melanie moved closer to Trent as he moved his hand to her upper thigh pushing her dress up. She felt his warm hand stroking her leg inching his fingers slowly up to her panties. He kissed her lips and neck. Melanie began to tremble with excitement and moaned. "Let's get out of here."

Lightning streaked across the sky as Trent followed her back to her apartment. Pulling into the parking lot, she stood outside her car as she watched him walk over to her. Melanie giggled to herself hoping he was as good in bed as he was on the dance floor. Thunder could be heard nearby warning them a storm was approaching. He took her into his arms and kissed her passionately. She could feel his hardness pressing into her as she spread her legs to give him easy access, letting him know she needed more. He pulled down her black laced panties stepping out of them as they fell to the ground. His hand began feeling her pussy, rubbing it gently sticking his warm fingers inside of her bringing her near climax. Pushing her dress up looking into her eyes, he paused.

"Are you okay with this?" He asked.

She was filled with desire for this man she hardly knew. It made him more desirable. "Don't stop," she whispered into his ear. She felt his sweet lips, leaving hers as he knelt down on the ground licking her between her legs. Her excitement growing as his tongue darted in and out until she couldn't stand it anymore. Grabbing his hair she pulled him up. "Take me now I need to feel you inside of me." He quickly pulled out a condom and put it on. Melanie spread her legs further as she felt him thrust himself deep inside of her. Damn did he feel good, as he pumped himself into her. Images of Eric came into her mind. Her whole body convulsed as she rode the explosion of ecstasy. He quickened his thrust throwing his head back shoving himself deeper into her as she moaned. Lightning continued to streak across the sky as the rain began to pour down on them. "We better get inside." She laughed as they made a run for her apartment.

THE BREAK IN

How dare Eric talk to her the way he did. She was up most of the night waiting for him to call her back and apologize. Or maybe he would come by and beg her forgiveness. But he didn't, and this made her angry. She would show him. The next day Becky drove to where Eric worked to make sure his car was there before continuing to his apartment where she had a copy of his key. He had never invited her over to his place but she had followed him home on several occasions without him knowing this. Two months earlier she noticed he had pulled up to his apartment, walked up to the door but didn't go in. He then went back to his car and reached under the driver's side and retrieved something and then continued back to his door. A few minutes later he came back out and put something back under his driver's side. Later, when she thought it was safe to look, she found a metal box with a magnet he had placed there. She looked inside and found a key. Eric must have misplaced his for him to come out and grab this one. She quickly went to the nearest hardware store and made a copy and then replaced the one he had. Now it was easy to come and go into Eric's place as she pleased. She was always very careful not to disturb anything that he might notice. Sometimes she would go there and imagine they lived together. She'd sit at the kitchen table and could see Eric sitting across from her. She would have candles burning, and they would be eating a fabulous dinner she had prepared. She would laugh out loud over something he said. He would tell her how wonderful she was and how much he loved her. She would always go through his drawers touching and smelling his clothes, being careful to replace anything exactly how he had it. This time she had gone into his desk where he had all of his important papers and bills. She came across a Visa debit card that was still good. He also had a sticky note attached to it with the numbers written two, three, seven four. This must be his pin, she thought.   Smiling to herself, she took the card and the note and slipped it into her wallet inside her purse. "Thank you sweetheart, I'll try not to spend too much money."   Becky quickly looked around making sure nothing was out of place before closing and locking the door behind her.

THE ENCOUNTER

Ted's funeral was tomorrow. Tony felt like going into town and took the car they had rented. He drove down the familiar road route fourteen to the stores in Crystal Lake. He spotted a big chain book store that would also sell coffee. He parked and walked in. The store was not busy and he went over to the science section and found a book that he liked. He purchased it and then went to the coffee shop and ordered an espresso with a doughnut. Sitting down he noticed a woman watching him who was sitting at another table. She looked strangely familiar. Shoulder length red hair, attractive, wearing a green shirt that matched her eyes and jeans. He was used to people recognizing him and figured as she stood up to approach him it was to ask for his autograph.

"You fucking son of a bitch." The red head yelled in anger as she threw her coffee into his face. "How dare you show yourself around here."

"Excuse me," Tony quickly grabbed a napkin to wipe his face. "Do I know you?" The red head's action had everyone watching.

"Go fuck yourself." The woman turned and started towards the door.

"Wait," Tony yelled to her getting up to follow. "You owe me an explanation. Who are you? You look familiar."

The red head stopped suddenly and turned to Tony. "I owe you an explanation?" The anger in her voice grew louder. "I owe you an explanation." Her green eyes glared back at him. "What is your explanation for what you did to Connie and Trisha? Get the fuck away from me you asshole." She turned to leave.

"Wait," he yelled following her out of the store. "Are you talking about Connie Wade? Who is Trisha? Now I remember you. Are you Lori, Connie's friend, right?"

"My name is Loretta you asshole. And I was Connie's friend up until she died."

"Oh my god, she died? When? I'm so sorry, I had no idea." Tony paused remembering how upset she was the last time he saw her. It wasn't suicide was it?"

"No, it was a car accident." Loretta was giving him a strange look. "You do know about Trisha don't you?"

"Who is Trisha? I don't remember her. Was she a friend of Connie's?" Tony watched as the red heads face turned to white and dropped the bag of books she was holding. "Are you okay," he asked. "Do you need to sit down?" Tony picked up her bag and handed it to her.

"I think you're the one that will need to sit down for this one," her voice no longer sounding angry. "And you might want something stronger than a cup of coffee. Follow me to Dukes Alehouse across town. "I'll buy you a drink."

Tony pulled out behind Loretta as they drove down route fourteen turning right onto South Main Street which led into the older part of Crystal Lake. After crossing the railroad tracks they parked their cars and walked into the bar and sat at a table by the window. The place was empty except for the bartender and a man who was watching a sports channel on the television on the wall. Tony ordered a shot of brandy and a beer. Loretta ordered a Strawberry Daiquiri. She waited for the drinks to arrive before starting the conversation. "By the way, I'm sorry about spilling the coffee on you. I owe you a new shirt. I didn't burn you did I?"

Tony looked down to see the coffee stain. "No, I'm okay. It really wasn't hot."

"When was the last time you talked to Connie?" Loretta asked.

Tony drank the brandy and sat back in his chair running his hand through his hair trying to remember. "I think it was the day after the band got signed. Geez Loretta, you are talking some twenty-four years ago. I'm not sure, I remember her telling me she was pregnant and she was going to get an abortion."

Loretta took a big sip of her drink. "Well she didn't have an abortion." Loretta lifted her glass for a toast, "congratulations you're the biological father of a twenty three year old girl. And her name is Trisha."

Now it was Tony's face that turned white. "I'm a Father?" His eyes widened, "bartender, I'll have another shot please."

Loretta waited till Tony finished off his shot. "Well I wouldn't exactly call you that. Connie married Rick and he adopted Trisha when she was young. He raised her and I have to admit did a great job. After the car accident, it was really hard on him when Connie died. There was a bad snow storm and she was on her way home from Christmas shopping when some drunk driver plowed into her. She died at the hospital. He started drinking heavily and he had us all worried. He loved her so much." Loretta's eyes began to tear, as she shook her head. "I thought her death was going to put an end to him. Trisha was only seven when that happened, but somehow she pulled him through. They have been close ever since. Rick remarried sometime back. Has two teenage boys now."

"What about Trisha?" Tony asked.

"She is doing great. She is a veterinarian in Woodstock. That girl loves horses." Loretta laughed finishing her drink and ordering them two more.

Tony was suddenly filled with pride and joy for a daughter he had never met or knew existed. "I have to meet her," he said smiling. "I'm sure you heard our drummer Ted passed away. We are here for the funeral which is tomorrow. But hearing this news, I want to stay and meet her, I have too. I can't wait, when can you set it up?" Tony signaled the bartender to bring over two more drinks.

"Wait a minute here, Tony. You have to realize you are about twenty-three years too late. She is fully aware of who you are and does not want anything to do with you. No, no, no," Loretta shook her head. "That is not going to happen. It would be best if you go back to your rock and roll world in which you came from. Forget I said anything. Trisha is so happy and knows what her goals are. She does not need you to come into her life and fuck it up."

"Please Loretta," he begged. "I know I fucked up big time. I know going on the road and leaving Connie when she needed me was the biggest mistake of my life. By the time I tried calling her she changed her phone number. Back then I couldn't find her and too quickly gave up. And you say she married so that is probably why I couldn't find her online. Her last name changed. I was young and stupid, I will admit it. I've always regretted what I did. Will you at least ask her?"

Loretta finished her drink, "I don't know Tony, all those years seeing your name splashed across the tabloids, seeing you with different woman. She hates you for how you treated her mother and her. And I can't blame her for that." Loretta's green eyes met his. "It's about the lowest thing a person could do."

Tony sat silently for a few minutes taking the information in. "You know I have a right to be upset here too. No one bothered to call me up and say, hey dude you have a daughter. It would have been easy to find me. I could of helped pay for her car, education, anything she wanted. I missed out on all that and more." Tony was hoping his point was getting across to Loretta.

"You never got married? No kids? Loretta asked.

Tony looked down at his beer. "No, I never thought being on the road was a good way of raising a family. I've seen what my band mates have gone through, drinking, drugs, partying and their marriages usually end in divorce, seeing their kids maybe once a year. It is a far different lifestyle than the typical suburban family. Do I regret it?" Tony shrugged his shoulders. "I don't know. I do know I'm lonely. I have no family photos in my home, no family to call at Christmas or birthdays. Oh geez, don't listen to me, I've had too many shots."

Loretta sighed, and reached into her purse and took out a pen and paper and slid it across the table. "Give me your phone number and I'll see what I can do. I can't promise anything so don't get your hopes up."

"Thank you Loretta," he said writing down his phone number and address and handing it back to her as she stood up to leave. "Please call me one way or the other, okay?"

Loretta smiled, "I'll give you a call."

Tony stayed for one more shot and walked back to the rental and drove back to the hotel. His mind was reeling with his conversation with Loretta. God, he hoped she could convince Trisha to call him. What should he say to her? Did she like his band? Probably not, remembering Loretta stating Trisha hated him. What kind of music did she like? Did she look like him?

Tony walked into the hotel lobby seeing the guys at a table eating dinner. He walked over and sat down.

"Where the fuck have you been?" Steve asked. "You have been gone a long time."

Tony grinned, "I'm a Father. Can you believe it, I'm a Father."

Alex looked at Danny and Steve and then Tony. "Dude, you haven't been gone that long."

"Steve and I were just talking about this on the plane. Her name was Connie and we dated like twenty-four years ago. She got pregnant and I thought she had an abortion. Turns out she didn't. I ran into her friend at the book store and we went and had some drinks and she told me I have a daughter. She also told me Connie died in a car accident when her little girl was seven."

"I don't know dude. How do you know this girl is really your daughter? I've had a woman say she was pregnant and it was mine. But I know I didn't even fuck her. It might be a scam to get money from you."

Tony shook his head. "Connie wasn't like that. She wasn't a one night stand. We had a thing. And if this was scam to get money, someone would have come after me years ago. She knows who I am. Anyways, it sounds like she won't have anything to do with me. According to Loretta, Trisha hates me for what I did to her Mother. She is now twenty-three years old and a veterinarian working at a nearby clinic.

The waitress came to the table with food and asked Tony what he wanted. Noticing the thick steak she put down in front of Danny, he ordered the same and a cup of coffee.

"So what are you going to do?" Alex asked taking a bite of his spaghetti.

"I would like to hang around here for a few days instead of going back to Palm Springs. I gave my phone number to Loretta hoping she can convince Trisha to call me."

"Well you do what you have to do bro." Danny said wiping his mouth with the napkin. "The plan is we are catching the seven P.M. flight back to Palm Springs the day after Ted's funeral."

"I know, I should call Eric and let him know I'm staying a few extra days. He can handle the club while I'm gone. I already rescheduled most of the recording sessions." The waitress returned with his steak and placed it down in front of him. He took a bite, "this is good." After dinner they sat in the lounge area drinking and talking about the good old days. Tony felt an ache in his heart when the conversation would turn to Ted. "I'm really going to miss that guy."

TED'S FUNERAL

The sky was over cast with clouds and the air was damp and chilly. Reporters and fans were waiting outside the church when the limousine pulled up. Ted's family had hired a security team to maintain privacy inside the church and the burial would be at a later time. The family did not want the public to find out where Ted was to be buried. Three tall well built men in suits were there to open the car doors yelling to the reporters to step back. They could not keep the flashes from the cameras from going off. They were quickly escorted inside where silence engulfed them. People who were seated in the pews quickly turned to watch the remaining four Quick Shots walk in. Tony was the last in line to approach the casket. On each side stood a huge array of flower arrangements and photos taken over the years of Ted from the time he was a baby to most recent.

"It is the only time I think I've ever seen Ted in a suit," Danny commented.

Upon looking into the casket, Tony swallowed hard as he tried to hold back tears. "I love you bro," he whispered as he looked down on his friend.

"Hey look," Alex said pointing to a photo frame that sat on a nearby table. "This was taken the first night Mike O'day came to hear us and said he wanted us to sign with Tri Recording."

Tony looked at the photo and smiled. It showed all five of them standing proudly on stage with Mike O'day and the owner of the lounge whose name he could not remember. But he did remember watching Connie on the dance floor, seeing her face turn white as she fell into her friend Sam's arms and passing out. Tony quickly got off stage and went to her side. The dance floor cleared and the manager came up to see what was going on. Alex coming up saying "I want this thing taken care of fast and get back on stage." He remembered telling Connie he would be with her as soon as he could before Loretta took her home. Instead he partied after the show back at Ted's, not showing up until the next evening still drunk with no sleep. The memory of Connie telling him the shocking news that she was pregnant. "God what a fucking idiot I was," Tony said out loud.

"It was a long time ago my friend." Alex patted Tony on his back as if reading his thoughts. "We all make mistakes."

Wanda, who was a tall attractive woman with short blonde hair and dressed in a slim black dress, approached the guys after they stepped away from the casket. "I want to thank you for coming" her eyes red from crying. "I can't tell you how much this means to me and his family." Wanda looked towards the first few isles. Tony recognized the group of nine to be Ted's children. They stood together like a clan. Tony guessed their ages from about ten to twenty-five. Most of them from different woman he had sex with over the years.

"I know he loved you guys so much." She pointed over to a couple of acoustic guitars sitting in the corner. "Whenever you would like to start is fine." She had asked Alex if they would like to play something before the service. Everyone had agreed Ted would have liked that. Steve sat at the piano and Danny and Tony grabbed a guitar and tuned them before taking a chair next to Alex who would keep rhythm tapping his hands on a guitar case and shaking a container of Tic Tacs.

Tony cleared his throat, "Ted was our drummer but most of all he was our friend. This one is for you bro." The guys started to play Amazing Grace, Tony sang with such emotion, you could see tears in everyone's eyes. Boxes of Kleenex were being passed around. They did two more songs and then the Pastor stood before Ted's coffin and recited verses from the bible.

"We will ask Ted's friends and then his family to say good-bye to him," the Pastor said. "Then everyone is welcome to have lunch at Ted's family home. Maps will be passed out."

People stood up and began to form a line to say good-bye to Ted. Suddenly two women standing next to Ted's coffin began to yell. Tony recognized Veronica and Yvette, and knew they were both bombed out of their minds. They were the groupies that would often follow the band on the long road trips when the wives or significant other didn't come along. The tall midsize woman in her forties with curly brown hair dressed in a tight short black dress was Veronica. She grabbed onto the coffin to steady herself. "Ted never loved you," she slurred. "You were nothing but a whore to him."

"A whore, you are calling me a whore?" Yvette, who was the dishwater blonde dressed in a black pants outfit and a purple low cut top revealing her size D breast implants slurred back. "I'm not the one that made national news by getting kicked out of a club for sucking the bands winkies under the table."

"I was not sucking their winkies." The brunette yelled back. "I dropped my phone and was trying to retrieve it."

"And I suppose that was the clubs special white sauce you had all over your face."

"You bitch."

"You cunt."

The two women began throwing punches and pulling each other's hair at the same time bumping into Ted's coffin sending it teetering back and forth until finally it fell, sending them to the floor with Ted lying on top of them both. Flower arrangements on each side also fell, sending petals into the air.

A photographer who had sneaked in quickly ran to the scene and began snapping photos of Veronica lying face up with her make-up smeared and her leg in the air and Yvette, lying on her with Ted on top of both of them.

"That is amazing; Ted's winkie is still getting him into trouble." Alex said.

All four of them began laughing uncontrollably.

Veronica tried to move from under Yvette and Ted. "Get off of me bitch."

The funeral director along with two of his associates quickly turned the coffin over and placed Ted back in. Tony saw there was now a smile on Ted's face. Veronica and Yvette noticed it also as they stumbled to their feet with the help of two of Ted's boys.

"Oh look, we made Teddy smile." Yvette slurred, looking into the coffin as she stuffed her right boob back into her shirt that fell out during the mishap.

"I do believe he was trying to say good-bye to us. Wouldn't you agree?" Veronica asked dabbing her eyes with a Kleenex.

"Most definitely," Yvette agreed looking down at Ted.

Once outside the funeral home, reporters rushed towards them asking questions and taking photos. Security men kept them at bay as the remaining four Quick Shots got into the limousine. Tony handed the driver the map through a connecting window from the back seat with directions to where the gathering would resume. "Try to lose the press." He sat back in his seat and took the small bottle of whiskey Danny handed him. "To Ted," Tony said holding up his drink before downing the bottle.

"To Ted," Alex, Danny and Steve chimed in. Forty Minutes later they pulled up in front of a large two story home set on an acre. Cars packed the driveway and the street.

"Do you know whose house this is?" Steve asked.

"Have no idea." Tony said following his band mates up the walk and into the house. The house was full of people that were at the funeral. Ted's clan of children could be seen standing silently together in the corner of the living room next to the brick fireplace.

Alex followed Tony's gaze. "They are kind of creepy aren't they? It's like they are glued together or something."

Tony smiled, "I bet half of his kids came from his triple double nights that he had after a show."

Alex laughed, "Isn't it a term used in basketball?"

"Yeah but Ted's version meant he had been with two women three nights in a row or three women two nights in a row."

"I remember those nights." Danny laughed. "Those were pretty wild times."

Alex laughed, "I'm surprised his so called winkie didn't fall off from all the fucking he did."

Steve shook his head. "I'm going to get something to drink." Steve walked down the hallway and was stopped by an attractive tall blonde woman who appeared to be in her early thirties wearing a tight gray dress.

"You are one of the band members." She said leaning into him holding a drink in her right hand.

"That would be me." Steve smiled back. "Maybe you can help me find something to drink around here?"

The tall blonde smiled back, "I can find you that and more." She took his hand leading him down the hall opening up into a kitchen where more people stood around engaged in conversation. On a counter in the middle of the room was a make shift bar. Bottles of wine, whiskey, vodka and more were placed next to a stack of plastic cups. "Help yourself," she said pouring herself another one as she leaned against the counter.

Steve made himself a rum and coke. "So, how did you know Ted?"

"He was my cousin. My mother and his were sisters."

Tony, Alex and Danny entered the kitchen and joined Steve at the counter pouring themselves drinks. A group of four women that were standing on the other side of the kitchen came over and surrounded them.

Tony knew the scene. They would all get drunk and before the night was over, he and his friends would find a room where the private parties would begin. But tonight he wasn't in the mood. He finished his drink. "I think I'm going to head back to my room," he told the others.

"Are you sure you don't want to stick around?" Alex said in a low voice. "This could be like the old days if you know what I mean."

"I'm sure it will be," Tony said. "Have fun and I'll see you guys later." Steve, Alex and Danny said good-bye as he left. He got into the limo that brought them there and went back to the hotel and watched television before falling asleep.

It was mid afternoon the next day when Steve, Alex and Danny returned to the hotel to pack. They met in the café located in the hotel on the first floor. Tony could see they were hung over and drained from the previous night of partying. "You guys can't handle it like you used too. Time we realized it, we are getting old." Tony teased.

"Speak for yourself." Danny smiled.

"You should have stayed." Alex said taking a sip of his coffee. "You missed out."

"That blonde Ted's cousin, wow she was hot." Steve said, "it must run in the family."

Tony called the car rental place and told them he would be staying a week longer, maybe two. The same limo driver came to take Danny, Alex, Steve to the Milwaukee airport to catch their flight back to California.

Danny hugged Tony, "hope she calls you man. Let us know what happens."

"Let's get together when you get home." Alex said giving Tony a hug before getting into the limo.

Tony gave Steve a hug and watched his friends pull away. He went back up to his room and fell asleep. It was around nine when the ringing from his cell phone woke him up. It was not a number he recognized and almost let it go to voice mail, but answered it anyways.

"Hi Tony, it is me Loretta."

"Tony held his breath in anticipation. "Hi, did you talk to Trisha?"

"Yes I did. I'm sorry Tony. She really is not interested in meeting you. I told her how you didn't know about her till a few days ago, but it didn't seem to make a difference. I did my best."

Tony's heart sank with despair. "Well I'm not going to give up just yet. I've planned on staying in town for maybe two more weeks, maybe I can change her mind. You said she is a vet, where does she work?"

There was apprehension in her voice. "I don't know if giving you that information is a good idea. What do you plan on doing? Walking in and announcing who you are? She would recognize you in a minute. Your recent photos hit the local papers when your drummer died and it was announced the funeral would be in Woodstock. She will have your ass thrown out in a minute."

"What if you offer to take her out to lunch and I show up?"

"Look, this is something I don't think I should get involved in. I did what you asked of me. I went to her and told her what you said. She is not interested and I think you need to accept this. And Rick raised her and is her father. His feelings should be considered in all of this as well."

"You are right, I should talk to him first."

"No," Loretta stated sternly. "You are not listening to me. These people are my family. I love them. Connie was my sister as well as my best friend. My parents took her in when her own parents died. I'm not going to let you come in and disrupt their lives like this. Go home Tony, go back to California."

Tony held the phone to his ear letting Loretta's words sink in as he ran his hand through his hair with the other staring at the floor. "I can't, I just can't."

"Then you are on your own." Loretta said before hitting the end call on her cell.

Tony hung up the phone feeling depressed. He was not expecting Trisha to say no, about meeting him. Now what, he thought to himself. Should he go home, should he try to contact her himself? He fell asleep with no answer.

PRACTICE

It was early afternoon and Melanie had just returned to work from lunch when her cell phone rang. Looking at her caller ID she saw it was Eric. "Hello," she answered.

"Look, I was wondering if we could get together tonight and go over a few of the songs? There were a few we didn't play last weekend because we had not gone over them yet."

"Sure, where do you want to meet?"

"How about we practice at your place? That way you don't have to drag your keyboard out and I'll bring my acoustic. What time is good for you?"

Melanie looked at her schedule on her desk. Her last appointment was at four. A couple was coming in to plan their honeymoon trip. "Seven works for me."

"Good, I'll stop and get a pizza and that way we can work and eat at the same time. What is your address?"

Melanie gave it to him and felt a surge of excitement at the idea of Eric coming over. She quickly reminded herself this was strictly to rehearse. "Sounds good, I like pepperoni by the way. I'll see you then." Melanie was trying to keep her cool. Her four o'clock clients had arrived late and now could not decide on whether to spend their honeymoon in Fiji or Hawaii Islands. He wanted Fiji and she was insisting on Hawaii. The time was now after five and everyone else in the office had left for the day. It would be a mad dash for her to get ready before Eric arrived. "Here is what I think you should do." She said to the couple who were in their thirties seated in front of her desk. "Why don't you look through the two packages I have given you? Take it home, look at them, talk it over, and sleep on it. I want you to be happy, this is your honeymoon. Something you will remember and talk about the rest of your lives." Melanie stood up to indicate to the couple it was time to go. "I'm really sorry we can't work on this more right now, but I have a seven o'clock appointment."

"Oh we are so sorry." The man said standing up. "We didn't realize it was so late." He scooped up the two packages off the desk and looked at his fiancé who seemed irritated by the sudden rush to leave.

Melanie switched off her computer and walked towards the door. "I'll call you in a day or two to see what you decided." After the couple left she quickly grabbed her things and made sure all the lights were turned off. She then locked up and walked to her car. When she got home she quickly ran around picking up things and washing some dishes that were in the sink. She changed into a pair of jeans and a cool pink short sleeved shirt and applied fresh make-up and combed her hair. She then went to her piano and started playing a song she had been working on. It was a slow romantic ballad. It was five to seven when her doorbell rang. She opened her door to see Eric standing with his guitar case in one hand and a pizza in the other. His blue eyes held a hint of a smile towards her.

"Am I too early?" He asked following her into the apartment. He set down his guitar next to her piano and followed her into the kitchen placing the pizza on her table.

"No you are fine," she said grabbing two plates from her shelf. "I just had some clients that couldn't decide where to go for their honeymoon. So I was running late. No big deal. What would you like to drink? I have pop, wine, beer, water, coffee."

"Beer sounds good." Eric took a seat at the table looking around the room. "Nice place you have here."

"Thanks," she said handing him a beer and pouring herself a glass of wine and taking a seat at the table.

"I heard you playing just now. What was that song? I like it."

Melanie felt her face blush as she took a sip of her wine. "Oh, just something I've been working on."

"I like to hear more of it. If it sounds good, we can add it to the CD when we go back to recording."

Melanie swallowed her food and wiped her mouth with a napkin as she smiled. "Are you serious? You would consider putting one of my songs on your CD?"

Eric sat back in the chair. "Why not and why are you surprised?"

After they finished eating their pizza, Melanie walked over to the piano and started playing the song that Eric said he liked. When she was finished she was quiet, afraid to look at him to see his expression. Afraid she would see he was displeased.

"That was great," Eric said after a few minutes of silence. "Do you have the words written yet?"

"No not yet. You really like it?" Melanie felt relieved. She stood up and poured herself a glass of red wine. She also reached for another beer from the fridge for Eric.

"Yes, I do. I think it has great possibilities." Eric's phone began to ring and he looked at the caller ID. It was a new number that kept coming up. "Damn," he said not answering it and putting the phone back in his pocket. "I am sure it's Becky I can't get rid of her. That is like the tenth time she has called today. I'm going to change my number which sucks because all my club contacts have this number."

"I thought Shane did something to your phone so it wouldn't ring when she called?"

"She got around it by buying disposable phones so I don't recognize the numbers. I silence one number and another pops up. She must have twelve different phones. I wouldn't be surprised if she followed me here."

"Maybe if you would quit fucking her, she would leave you alone." Melanie noticed the surprised look on Eric's face. "I'm sorry, I shouldn't have said that. It is none of my business."

"I have quit fucking her. She has this idea that I'm hers. She is crazy, and it has gotten so out of hand I don't know how to handle it. She is actually getting scary. She leaves really weird messages. Like why are you doing this to me, call me I miss you, I will make a good wife for you. Enough about me, how did things go for you the other night, with that guy that was at the show?"

A slight smile came to Melanie's face as she took a sip of her wine. "I think we need to get back to work."

Eric's phone rang again. This time he answered it. Melanie listened to the conversation. Realizing it was not his stalker Becky calling this time.

"Don't worry, take your time. We are not in any hurry. In fact it will give us some more time to work on some more songs." Eric said looking at Melanie. Just give us a call when you are back in town." Eric turned off his phone this time. "This way we won't be interrupted anymore. That was Tony. He is staying longer in Illinois. He said something about some personal business." Eric moved over and sat next to Melanie at the piano. "You know that one song we do," Eric played a few bars.

"Yes, I know the one," Melanie said.

"I was wondering if you could add something to it with the keys, something jazzy."

"Like this?" Melanie played a few minor cords.

"Yeah," Eric said with excitement. "That's it, I like it."

BECKY

Becky stood outside near a tree watching Eric and Melanie. Her anger rising as she saw him get up and move over towards her by the piano. How dare he do this to her? And that Melanie, Becky imagined taking a hammer and pounding her hands with it, breaking all of her fingers. A feeling of satisfaction came over her at the thought of it. Maybe even take the hammer to that pretty little face. Eric wouldn't want anything more to do with her after she was crippled. Then Eric would know how much she loved him and come to her begging forgiveness. Then they would be happy again. She would be his and he would go back singing his love songs to her. A car pulled into the parking lot shinning the headlights on her. She quickly ducked behind a tree. She couldn't stand where she was any longer without being seen. She waited until the car turned off the headlights and watched as a tall man went inside. Becky quickly ran to her car and opened the trunk and took out the tire iron. She needed to remind Eric she wasn't going to put up with this kind of behavior. She looked around to make sure no one was around before running over to Eric's car. She then raised the tire iron over her head coming down fast and hard smashing the glass in his rear window. As soon as she made contact, the car alarm went off. That will end their evening, Becky thought. She quickly ran to her car, throwing the tire iron into her back seat before driving away.

THE ALARM

Eric and Melanie heard the sound of glass breaking and a car alarm going off. Melanie quickly walked over to her patio window and saw a cars lights flashing on and off. "Eric, I think it is your car."

Eric went to where Melanie stood and looked into the parking lot. "What the fuck?" He then opened the sliding glass door and ran to his car. Melanie followed a few steps behind. Eric saw the glass on the pavement from his rear window being smashed out.

"What happened to your car?" Melanie stood next to Eric in shock.

"What's going on out here?" A neighbor of Melanie's yelled out as he stood in the doorway. The man hesitated if he should come out or not.

Melanie turned recognizing Jack who lived two doors down in apartment C. "Someone smashed my friend's car."

Jack now walked out of the building towards Melanie. "I saw a woman's standing over by that tree when I pulled up just a little while ago." Jack pointed to the area outside Melanie's apartment. "She was tall and thin and I think blonde. I thought it was weird her just standing there. When I got out of my car she was gone."

Eric looked at Melanie. "Damn that bitch Becky." Eric took out his cell phone and dialed a number. "What the fuck is wrong with you?" He yelled into the phone. Are you that insane? You need to stay away from me bitch. I'm calling the police so you can expect a visit from them. I'm pressing charges and you are going to pay for the damage you did to my car."

"I don't know what you are talking about sweetie. You sound upset. What is wrong?"

"Don't give me your bull shit, Becky. We have a witness that saw you outside Melanie's apartment."

"Now wait a minute," Jack said hearing the conversation. "I didn't see the person that did this." Jack pointed to the broken glass. "And I didn't get a good look at the woman."

"Why don't you come over here and we can talk about it." Becky cooed into the phone.

Eric hung up on her and then dialed 911.

"What is your emergency?" The dispatcher asked.

"Yes, I want to report a psycho bitch that is stalking me. She did damage to my car." Eric looked at Melanie.

"What is your address?"

He gave it to the dispatcher along with his name and hung up the phone. "They are on the way."

"She knows where I live," Melanie said with concern. "Is she crazy enough to come after me or you? She had to of been standing out here watching us Eric."

"I don't know what she is capable of. This just blows my mind. Maybe I should spend the night just in case she comes back." Eric said with a grin, his humor returning.

Melanie smiled back. "I don't think we need to go that far. But thanks for the offer."

The police pulled up with their lights flashing. Two officers got out of the car and inspected the damage. Jack the neighbor told them he saw a tall woman standing around outside Melanie's window but did not see who broke the car window. The officers said they would talk to Becky but could not file any charges without an eye witness. After the police left, Jack the neighbor went inside and Eric and Melanie proceeded to clean up the glass. "I'll call my insurance company tomorrow. I'm really sorry about all of this." Eric walked Melanie back to her apartment. "Are you sure you don't want me to spend the night?"

"I'm sure. Let me know when you want to get together again and finish up on the songs."

"Sounds good, I'll call you tomorrow and don't forget starting time for this Saturday is at eight instead of the usual nine. So load in will be at seven. Call your brother and remind him please. I have a feeling I'm going to be busy taking care of my car."

"If you need a ride anywhere, let me know."

"Thanks, I just might. Good night Melanie." Eric went to his car and got in behind the wheel. Hoping there would not be any surprises when he got home.

He cautiously unlocked his door and proceeded to turn on lights in his apartment. He was getting an eerie feeling lately when he came home. Even though things looked to be the same, his guard was up, especially tonight. He walked slowly from room to room. He didn't want to alarm Melanie, but he was becoming fearful of Becky. He had met her at one of his shows months ago. She came over to him and introduced herself. That first night, he thought she was beautiful and was turned on by her outfit. She wore a short blue jean skirt that showed off her long tan legs. Watching her on the dance floor with her moves made him hard. He didn't hesitate when she invited him back to her place. She didn't disappoint him. She quickly went down on him as soon as she closed her door. Telling him she couldn't wait to taste him. Then stripping off her own clothes and leading him to her bedroom. Telling him she had to feel him inside of her now. He remembered thinking, wow, this chick is wild. She would always try to get him to stay but he never did. Now with all the phone calls from her and texts she must be insane. She had to of followed him to Melanie's, and breaking his window like that. Once in bed after checking to make sure all the windows were locked, Eric climbed into bed only too toss and turn. It was late before he finally fell asleep.

The next morning he called his insurance company and they told him where to get his car repaired. He made an appointment and went off to work. He called Melanie on his break to make sure things were okay with her. After hearing from her nothing out of the ordinary had happened after he left, he began to relax. Maybe Becky just needed to let off some steam. But it was a crazy way to do it. He was sure the police had talked to her. She probably wouldn't try anything else after last night. He was looking forward to playing the next gig and seeing Melanie again. She was so easy to talk to. And she understood and had the same love for music that he did. The tune she had written went through his mind. He could add some really cool cords to her song and it would sound great. Next they could work on the lyrics. He was done going over the staff schedule for next month and posted it on the board. He was done for the day and after saying goodnight to everyone, he walked to his car and saw Becky dressed in her usual low cut blouse and mini skirt leaning against his car. She smiled as he approached her.

"What the fuck are you doing here?"   He felt his anger starting to rise. Eric quickly walked around his car to see if she had done any more damage.

"I want you to know I would never do anything to hurt you. I don't understand why the police came to my door last night. That is why I am here. I thought something might have happened to you. I was worried. They said someone smashed your car window. Are you okay?"

Eric looked at Becky suspiciously.   Could he be wrong to accuse her? Melanie's neighbor said he didn't see who broke his window. Only gave a description of someone that sounded like Becky standing outside Melanie's window. Was she lying? If she did have something to do with this, she was putting on a good show. He couldn't see her eyes. She was wearing sun glasses, leaning on the driver's side door. "I'm fine, now if you don't mind moving, I need to go home."

"Even though you are accusing me of something I didn't do, I would be willing to loan you the money to help get this fixed."

"I am fine. I don't need your money. My insurance will cover most of it. Now please move and please quit calling and texting me." Eric said just wanting to get away from her.

Becky stepped away from the car and put her hands on her hips. Eric quickly got in behind the wheel and started his car.

"You owe me an apology Eric."   She yelled as he pulled away from her.

BECKY' PLANS

Becky watched Eric pull out of the parking lot and laughed. She had done an excellent job convincing him she had nothing to do with it. Just seeing Eric and talking with him brightened her mood. Now she just had to take care of that bitch Melanie and Eric would be running back to her in no time begging forgiveness. She would be more careful next time she paid a visit to the bitch's place. She would wear a disguise, maybe dress like a man. Just in case someone sees her. She had all kinds of fun ideas for Melanie. She could easily get into her apartment and taint her food with poison. Or somehow tie her up and drop off in a very bad neighborhood and let the gang bangers have fun raping her. She would like to see that happen. Maybe she could fuck around with her brakes and chase her off a cliff. There were so many tantalizing ideas she had. Poor little Melanie, she had no idea what was in store for her. No matter which plan she chose, she needed a disguise. Becky drove to the mall and found a parking space close to the entrance. She then walked into her favorite store. The man looked up and smiled.

"Hello and how are you today?" The short man with gray hair and glasses stood behind the glass counter.

"Very well, thank you. I'm here to look at wedding rings."

"Of course," the man smiled and went over to the glass case that held several rows of sparkling diamond rings in all shapes and sizes. Becky stood and stared closely looking at each one until her eyes came to an engagement ring that was a beautiful 14k gold band with an oval one ct. diamond set between smaller three diamonds on each side. It had a matching wedding band for the woman as well as a matching wedding band for the man. "This is the one," she quickly slipped on the wedding band and then the engagement ring over her finger and held up her hand and smiled, "it is perfect."

"This set is five thousand, and is worth every penny. If I may say, you have lovely hands and it looks like this set was made for you. When will your fiancé be coming in to see what you have picked out?"

Becky took out Eric's card from her wallet that she had taken from his desk and handed it to the man. "She smiled, "my fiancé told me to go buy whatever makes me happy. And this makes me happy." Eric won't mind she thought. Once he sees how beautiful the set is, he will realize it was the right choice. The salesman took the ring and put it in a blue box giving her another box for hers. "I think I'll leave mine on for now." Becky followed the man over to the cashier and watched as he swiped the card. She entered the pin that she had memorized and signed it Eric Maxwell and waited for it to go through.

"If there are any problems with it fitting your fiancés finger, have him bring it in and we can size it correctly. Have you set the date for the wedding?" The man asked as he handed her the receipt.

"No I have not," she corrected herself. "I mean we have not decided on a date yet."

"Well congratulations and I wish you the best of luck."

Her emotions made her feel like she was on a rollercoaster. The excitement was building inside of her. Now she needed to find a wedding dress. She knew of three bridal shops in the mall. The first one she walked into didn't have anything appealing. But the second store was larger and had a better selection.

A heavy set woman to be a bout forty years old with short hair came up to Becky. "Can I help you?"

"Yes," she smiled. "I just got engaged," Becky showed the woman her rings. "I know I shouldn't wear the wedding band until the day but I simply have too. It is so beautiful isn't it?"

"Oh it is." The sales lady agreed looking at Becky's hand. When is the date?"

"Soon, we can't wait. My fiancée is a very talented musician. He plays guitar and has his own band. He has several recording companies interested in his work. Maybe you have heard of him, Eric Maxwell?"

"No honey, I'm afraid I don't keep up with that kind of stuff. But it sounds very exciting for both of you."

"Well, I'm sure you have heard of Tony Sands from the Quick Shots? They were very big about twenty five years ago. They toured the country and Europe and their drummer just died."

"The Quick Shots, I remember. I use to listen to their songs all the time. Tony Sands was the lead singer, right?"

"Yes, he was. My fiancée is very close to him." Becky smiled as she nodded to the lady. In fact he is coming to our wedding. I hear he is writing a special song just for us, can you believe that? We told him he didn't have to, but Tony insists. He is so happy for us."

"Well, let us see what we can find to make you happy." The woman took down a beautiful white gown with sequins off the rack to show Becky. "I will look for more while you try this one on. The fitting rooms are in the back of the store."

Becky giggled with excitement as she headed towards the dressing rooms. It fit her perfectly. She always had a good figure. And the low cut in front showed off her cleavage.

The saleslady knocked on the door. "I have two more if you would like to try these on."

Becky opened the door and walked past the sales lady over to the three way mirror. She imagined walking down the aisle of a church towards Eric. "I want this one."

"The saleslady stood holding two more dresses. Maybe you would like to try on these two…"

"I said I want this one." Becky said loudly so the whole store could hear. "You just don't get it do you? If you don't want my business I can go somewhere else."

The saleslady stammered. "Of course, I'm so sorry. This one looks so beautiful on you. I'm sure your fiancé will agree."

A smile replaced Becky's glare. "You do understand. It is all about making him happy." She walked back to the dressing room and gently removed the dress. The saleslady took it from her and walked into the back room to have it boxed.

"What was that all about?" The manager whispered following the saleslady into the back room.

"I know did you see the look on her face? All I did was suggest she try on a few more dresses. I thought she was going to get ballistic on me. Just ring her up and get her out of here. That woman is crazy."

The manager nodded and took the boxed dress out to the cash register.

Becky took out Eric's card and swiped it into the machine, entering the pin and signing it. The authorization went through like it did with the rings.

"Thank you and I hope you have a wonderful wedding." The manager smiled as she handed her the receipt and the box.

"Thank you," Becky smiled back. "And you have a wonderful day." The next thing to do was to make plans for the honeymoon. And she knew just where to go. Becky's cell phone began to ring from her purse. She stopped walking and set down her bag to retrieve her phone. The number on the display told her it was her Aunt Patricia, her father's sister. She pressed the green button on her phone and said "hello."

"Hello my dear, I hope I'm not interrupting anything." The old woman's voice cracked on the other end.

"What is it Aunt Patricia, I'm very busy I have my wedding to plan."

"Yes I know dear, and you're Father and I can't wait to meet him. You know, before the wedding. What about bringing him out this weekend? We will have a lovely time."

"I'm afraid that is not possible. Eric has a busy schedule. He is booked every weekend. And he is working on new songs."

"Becky you really need to come home and visit. Your Father misses you so much, we both do. We will have dinner at the country club."

"How is Father?" She asked trying to change the subject. Becky knew what this phone call was about.

She shouldn't have answered it. They didn't want her to have a life. They didn't want her to be happy. They locked her up in a mental institution for two years and tried to convince her that she was crazy. They told her she never had a strong mind, and needed to be put on medication to help with what they called hallucinations. It was all an excuse so her father could have her out of his way so he could be with his girlfriends. None of them liked her. There were a few that tried to be a mother to her. But then she realized it was all an act, an act for her father. So maybe he would marry them and they would become Mrs. Sheldon of Sheldon Industries. They all would make up stories to her father about her.

"Becky, I was hoping our conversation wouldn't go this way. We have talked to Dr. O'keefe and she has said you have not been keeping your appointments with her. I hope you are still taking your medication. I've made an appointment for you with her for Monday morning at ten a.m. If you don't keep in touch with Dr. O'keefe you give us no choice but to cut your allowance. And either you can move back here with us or go back to the hospital. It is your choice."

"Fine, I will go Monday and see her."

"And will you be coming home to visit with us this weekend?"

"Alright, I will," Becky said gritting her teeth. "I have to go now. I will see you this weekend." Becky hung up the phone. "Damn, that fucking bitch. I hate her," she raged. A few people stopped to turn and looked at her. "What the fuck are you staring at?" Becky screamed at them. More people were pointing and began whispering her name. Becky, Becky. "How do you know my name?" She yelled out loud. She put her hands over her ears so she wouldn't hear them, but it was no use. She had to get out of the mall. She picked up her bag and quickly headed towards the parking lot. Were they following her? "Leave me alone, leave me alone."

When she got to her car, she threw her package with the gown in the back seat and started the car and pulled away nearly hitting a woman walking towards the mall with a little girl. "You fucking bitch," Becky yelled at her. "Get out of my way."

The woman quickly grabbed the little girl and stared in disbelief at Becky.

THE MEETING

Tony called and found the veterinarian hospital where Trisha worked. It wasn't hard to find. There were only two veterinarian hospitals for Woodstock. Next he went to a nearby florist and picked out a beautiful array of a dozen red roses and a dozen pink carnations mixed together. He wrote a note, To Trisha, please do me the honor of having dinner with me tomorrow evening at The Public House on the square at seven pm. I would very much like to meet you. I will be wearing a blue LA Dodgers cap in case you don't recognize me. He told the florist where to send it and paid for the flowers. It was a long shot, but he had to try. He made some phone calls and checked in with Eric at the club.

"Anything I should know about?" Tony asked.

"Business is great. The place has been packed every night. I hate to say this but I think all the press about Ted's death and the Quick Shots has brought in a lot of new customers. A number of people have asked about you. I think they are hoping to get a glimpse of the famous rock star Tony Sands. Even a reporter came in asking me about you. What is it like working for you? Do you have anyone special in your life? I said you are a great guy to work for. And that is about it. When are you coming back?"

"I'm not sure yet Eric. I've got something important going on here. I can't get into it now, but I will tell you all about it when I return." Hearing about the press coming into the club sent up a red flag. The press would be all over this story if they found out he just became aware of being a father.

He didn't want anyone to find out about Trisha. No doubt in his mind they would hunt Trisha down for an interview. He had to be careful. He had an early dinner and went back to his hotel room and watched television but his mind kept thinking about Trisha and what would he say if she comes to meet him tomorrow night. "Hi I'm your father and I'm sorry I wasn't there for you. I didn't know you existed. So how is life been for you?" Nothing sounded right. He began to get nervous. She probably thinks I'm an idiot. And she would be right. Maybe she won't show. What do I do if she doesn't?"

The next day he was on pins and needles. He did some shopping to break up the day. He picked up a couple of new pairs of jeans and shirts and underwear and socks. He had not planned on staying this long and didn't bring enough clothes. It was after five when he returned to the hotel. He had just enough time for a quick shower and change. He then drove to the square in Woodstock and found a parking place close by to the Public House. He wanted to get there early and get a seat so she could see him first if she came. The waitress showed him a table towards the back. And he ordered a scotch on the rocks to calm his nerves. She returned with his drink and asked if he was ready to order.

"I think I will wait." He smiled at the waitress and took a sip.

He was half way done with his drink when he saw her walk through the door. His heart skipped a beat. He knew in an instant it was her, Trisha. She looked just like her mother Connie. It was like stepping back in time, seeing Connie twenty-two years ago. She had her beautiful dark hair, ivory skin but her blue eyes were shaped like his. And he knew in his heart this was his child, his daughter. He was overwhelmed with emotion. She looked around the room resting her eyes on him in his blue baseball hat. He smiled holding back his tears and waved to her. She had come, he had his doubts that she would show. He watched as she slowly made her way towards him. He stood up and held the chair out for her wanting to hug her but knew that it would probably be uncomfortable for her. "Thank you for coming," he said as he took his seat across from her.

"Thank you for the flowers. They are beautiful."

"I didn't think you would come."

"Are you ready to order?" The waitress appeared with a pad of paper and pen in her hand.

"Please order something." Tony said. "I hear their loaded potato soup is delicious."

"Okay, I will have that and a coke please." Trisha said closing the menu and handing it back to the waitress.

"I will have the same," Tony said. "You look so much like your Mother. Loretta told me what happened, I'm so sorry. That must have been awful for you."

Trisha looked away, "I don't remember much about her. I was pretty young when she died."

The waitress came back with a coke and set it down on the table. "Would you like another drink?"

Tony wanted to say yes, but was afraid if he caught a buzz he would make a fool of himself. "No thank you, I will have a cup of coffee." He could see Trisha felt uncomfortable when he mentioned her Mother, and decided to change the subject. "I hear you're a veterinarian? That must keep you busy. How did you get into that?" The waitress returned with their soup and his coffee.

"Will there be anything else?"

"No thank you, how about you?" Tony asked Trisha.

"No, I'm fine," taking a sip of the soup. "This is good. After my mom died, my dad bought a horse ranch outside of Woodstock, Sundown Creek. Then he married Sue, my mom, I mean my step mom. She is also a veterinarian, one of the best in Mchenry County. That is how they met. She would come out to the ranch when one of our horses got sick. And they got married. My brothers and I were raised there. I couldn't see doing anything else. We were always tending to the animals." Trisha's eyes turned away from Tony's. "I loved that ranch. It was where my mom would go riding with my dad. I think that is why he bought it. He told me when I was little I ran away and he was frantic. He had woken up on a Saturday morning and I was gone. I had packed a bag and left in the middle of the night and walked all the way to Sundown Creek. He said that day changed his life forever. When we lost the ranch, it nearly destroyed him. Look, I have a busy day tomorrow," she said finishing her soup. "I just wanted to meet with you and thank you for the lovely flowers." She stood up to leave.

"Please, I'd like to see you again."

"You don't have to do this. I mean feel guilty or anything. My life turned out fine."

"It would mean a lot to me if we could stay in touch."

"Look Tony, I'd rather not have us stay in touch. As far as I'm concerned Rick is my father and that will never change. He would be terribly hurt if he knew I was talking to you. And I hope I never do anything in the world to hurt him. I hope you have a safe trip home, good-bye."

Tony was filled with different emotions as he watched Trisha walk out the door. Happiness to have met her and surprised and disappointed she still didn't want anything to do with him. Tony got the attention of his waitress and ordered another scotch on the rocks, his mind going over their conversation. Tony took out his cell phone and dialed Loretta's number. Third ring she answered.

"What do you want Tony?" Loretta's voice sounding irritated on the other end.

"I'm sorry to bother you again. I need to ask you something. Trisha just left a few minutes ago…

"What do you mean left? Where are you?"

"I'm at the Public House in Woodstock. I bought her dinner."

"So you met Trisha? Wow, I'm really surprised she agreed to meet you. She didn't sound at all interested when I talked to her. How did it go?"

"Look, why don't you meet me here. I'll buy you dinner too. If it were not for you I would have never of known about her. I owe you."

There was silence on the other end before Loretta spoke. "Sure, why not, I definitely want to hear this. But meet me at Angelo's across the square, I like their food there. I can be there in a half an hour. See you then."

Tony sat and waited finishing his drink and then walked across the street through the park to Angelo's. He was seated and ordered a cup of coffee and watched a family at a nearby table. They looked to be husband and wife with a small girl that sat next to the woman. Tony wondered what it would have been like to have a wife and children, someone to love. How would it feel to have someone to do things with? To share how his day went, someone to go places with. Most times he would order something they served at his club and sit and talk with the bartender Jen. If he went out to eat it was alone. His attention turned toward the door as he saw Loretta dressed in a soft brown sweater and jeans walk in. She brushed away a piece of her long red hair from her face as she looked around the room. Tony stood up and waived to her getting her attention. He waited for her to sit first and then sat down himself. The waitress appeared with a menu and handed it to Loretta.

"She looked over the menu, "everything here is good." She replied.

"Okay I'll have the ribs and coffee please." Loretta handed the menu back to the waitress and turned her attention to Tony. "So how did you get her to meet you? She seemed pretty persistent about not wanting to meet you when I last talked to her."

Tony smiled at Loretta. "I sent flowers to where she works asking if she would have dinner with me."

"Hmm, flowers huh? That's all it took?"

"Well I'm sure she was a little curious about me. She didn't stay long and asked that I not stay in touch with her. She said it would hurt her father if he found out. She also mentioned he lost his ranch where Trisha lived? What is that about?"

"Rick got laid off from his job and then unemployment ran out so they lost the ranch. His wife Sue makes good money being a vet but had a lot of the money invested over the years in Morgan horses. She had to find homes for them. It nearly destroyed her and Trisha having to get rid of them, especially Trisha. She had to sell her beloved Lightning. He was a beauty. Rick had given her that horse for her birthday one year." Loretta shook her head. "She loved that horse. I guess you can say Lightning and her grew up together." The waitress brought Loretta's food and coffee. And she began to eat. "This is really good. Would you like some?" She asked as she wiped her mouth with her napkin.

"No thank you, I already ate. I'm sorry to hear that." Tony said. It is such a tragedy that so many people are out of work and lost their homes. I sincerely doubt our country will recover from this economical upheaval, especially if we get a conservative in the white house for a president."

Loretta nodded her head in agreement. "I totally agree with you. I don't think most politicians care about the working class people. What they really want is control over the middle class. Oh don't get me started. I can go on all night when it comes to politics."

Tony laughed, "I better order more coffee. Did anyone ever tell you how beautiful you are when you get mad?"

"Oh you are a charmer." Loretta's cheeks grew red with embarrassment. "Now I see how you got Trisha to meet you." She said with a grin.

Tony laughed again. "Let us go for a walk in the square. I haven't been here in years."

Loretta pushed her plate away. "I have to tell you, nothing has changed. It is the same old town."

"Some things should never change. That is what I like about it." Tony took out money from his wallet and paid the waitress. "Keep the change," he said to her.

The waitress's eyes widened. "Thank you and hope you two have a nice evening."

"Thank you for dinner Tony."

"It was my pleasure." He turned and smiled at her. They walked out into the fresh cool air. Tony noticed it was now dusk and all the lanterns along the streets and in the park were lit.

"The town buildings were built in the late 1850's." Loretta said. "They were designed in a square that now face the park in the middle. A piece of history seems to stand still when you look around and see the old Opera House and the Courthouse along with other buildings. I often wonder what it was like to live here back then. I can just imagine people from the nearby farms coming to this town in horse and buggies to get their supplies or spend the evening at the Opera. If I could go back for just one day, I would."

Tony noticed a warm glow of lights coming from within the business's and stores as they stayed open. "Nice touch," looking down at the street paved with bricks. "Like I said, some things should never change." Tony said stepping off the curb walking towards the park.

"Don't you like," Loretta stopped. "Where is it that you live again?"

"Palm Springs California. And yes I do like living there. We have some beautiful canyons. But in summer it can get really hot." Tony sat down on a bench facing one of the gazebos. Loretta sat down next to him. "So what about you, is there a husband at home waiting for his dinner? Are there children that need to be tucked in?"

Loretta smiled and looked across the park. "No not anymore. I was married for three years. It was his second marriage. It just didn't work out. The problem was he was still in love with his first wife. After we divorced he married her again, can you believe that? I thought most people hated their ex spouses." Loretta shook her head, "I had no clue what was going on. I just knew I wasn't happy and he wasn't happy. When we split up, that is when everyone decided to come forward and tell me what they knew. Living in a small town isn't always a good thing. Everyone knows you. You can't escape that. Anyways, I'm over it and I'm happy living alone. I love my job, I'm a paralegal for the firm Perkins and Smith, and I don't have anyone else's laundry to do, or cook meals for. I can come and go as I please."

"I got you pegged now," Tony teased. On Saturday nights you like to hang out at the book store and wait for an unsuspecting gentleman to come in so you can throw coffee in his face. I have to tell you Loretta, that is some way to get a man's attention."

Loretta laughed. "Oh stop it. I only do that on Mondays." She grinned at Tony. So what is your plan now? Go home to Palm Springs I suppose."

Tony's face grew serious. "Yes, I will probably be leaving tomorrow."

"Well I should be getting home." Loretta stood up and so did Tony. "Don't worry about Trisha," she said. "She is a smart lady and Rick will always be good to her. She will be fine. I have to say I am glad we met. And I am sorry for throwing my coffee on you."

"It was my pleasure." Tony shook her hand. "You're a beautiful woman Loretta, inside and out. Thank you for your help."

Loretta smiled and turned and walked towards her car.

The next day Tony packed his bags and called the car rental place and told the man on the phone he would be dropping the car off at the airport where he would be catching his flight home. He checked out of his room and drove along the familiar country road figuring it would be a long time before he returned. He slowed down when he spotted an old sign. The paint was faded and some of it was chipped away. Weeds were now growing up around it. Tony could still read what it once said, Sundown Creek. Next to the older sign was a new one that read for sale 22 acres and at the bottom was a phone number. Tony continued driving past the sign thinking about what Trisha had said. How Rick had lost the ranch because of losing his job. Loretta's words about how Trisha had to give up her horse. Tony continued until the next driveway where he pulled in and turned around. He then turned into the long driveway that led to Sundown Creek. He parked the car and got out. He looked at the ranch house that now was empty. On the side was a huge barn that probably held the Morgan horses. A fenced in area surrounded the barn. Tony walked up to the house and peeked in the windows and saw a huge living area with a brick fire place and windows on each side facing the beautiful country side. A path that ran along a creek led into a thick forest. From there you could probably watch the horses in the coral. Tony could only imagine how hard it must have been to give up their home. He walked over to a nearby swing on the front porch and sat down. He pulled out his cell phone from his pocket and dialed Loretta's number.

"Hi, it's Tony, I was wondering if maybe you could help me with something?"

"I thought you were leaving to go home?"

"I am, or I was. I'm at Sundown Creek, are you busy right now? Can you meet here?"

"I'm at work, but I get off soon. What are you doing there?"

Tony took in a huge breath before speaking. "I will tell you when you get here. Just make it soon."

Tony spotted Loretta's car pulling up the driveway thirty minutes later. He watched as she stepped out of her car and noticed her red hair flowing in the breeze. She was wearing a short black skirt that showed off her tan legs with a matching black blazer. Tony thought how beautiful she looked. He yelled "over here by the barn." He watched as she gracefully walked towards him.

"What is this about," she asked. "What are you doing here? This is the ranch where Trisha and her Dad lived," she said looking out over the horizon.

"I know, I know. I was on my way to the airport when I saw the for sale sign. I want to buy it; I mean I want to buy it back for Trisha and Rick."

Loretta suddenly turned to Tony. "You would do that for her?" Tears formed in her eyes. "Why would you do that?"

Tony took Loretta into his arms and kissed her gently and looked into her eyes. "Because I want to, because I believe it would make her happy." He held Loretta in his arms and stroked her red hair. "I don't know anything about real estate. Will you help me make this happen?"

Loretta nodded. "First thing we better do is call the bank. They are the ones selling it. I'll set up an appointment for you. Do you know what the price is?"

"No, I don't have a clue." Tony smiled, "don't worry I'm sure I can afford it. I don't want Trisha and Rick to know until it is a done deal. And I want it in their names." Tony looked into her green eyes and wiped away her tears. "Stop crying this is a good thing."

"I know I can't believe you are doing this. It is wonderful. And all this time I thought you were such a jerk."

"Loretta I was, I will be the first one to admit it. But people can change. I was stupid and arrogant and selfish. I'm not that same guy that left Connie. I realize what I missed out on. And I will never be able to take back those years. I only wish I could. I would do things differently. You have to believe me."

Loretta nodded, "I do, let's go back to my office and get things started. The firm I work for handles real estate contracts so this should go smoothly.

Tony followed her back to her office and watched as Loretta made call after call regarding the sale of the ranch. He had cancelled his flight, called the car rental place and booked another week at the hotel he had stayed in.

"Goodnight Loretta," a short balding man wearing a tailored suit holding a briefcase said as he headed toward the main door. "Are you going to be staying late tonight?"

Loretta looked up from her desk and smiled. "Carl I would like you to meet my friend Tony. He is buying Sundown Creek. We will be handling the contract for him."

Carl walked over to Tony and shook his hand. "Good to meet you son. That is a nice place you are buying. I'm sure you will be very happy there."

"Well thank you sir, but I'm buying it for someone else. I won't be living there myself."

"Oh, I see." He looked over at Loretta. "Well you two have a nice evening. Don't forget to lock up my dear."

Loretta stood up and grabbed her purse from the drawer. "I think we are done for today. Goodnight Carl, I will see you in the morning." She smiled as she watched him close the door behind him. "He is such a great guy."

"Does he mainly do real estate contracts?"

"Now he does, he started out as a criminal lawyer. He had this one case where a young woman was murdered with a blunt object. They arrested this seventeen year old kid who till this day says he had nothing to do with it. I believe he was in the wrong place at the wrong time. Just happen to be walking home when the police got the 911 call from a neighbor saying she heard a woman screaming. The police got to the house and found the woman unconscious. Her face was beaten so badly she was unrecognizable. She died at the hospital and it was a closed coffin. A few days later, someone had told the police they saw Tommy McFarlen in the area about the time of the incident so they picked him up. He didn't stand a chance. They didn't even look at anyone else. The town was terrified that a killer was loose on the streets. So the Chief wanted to put everyone at ease by having them believe they had caught the right guy. And it would make him look good when it came election time. Anyways, Carl believed he was innocent but the jury convicted the kid. Carl felt it was his fault the boy was found guilty. He said there was never any proof Tommy had done this. No finger prints, no DNA, nothing found on Tommy or at his house. Carl couldn't believe the jury sent him away. And this being a small town, Carl knew half the jurors. Till this day he refuses to talk to anyone that was a juror on that case. He had a hard time dealing with it. He never took on another criminal case after that."

"I'm sorry that happened." Tony said as they walked out of the office. Loretta turned and inserted a key into the door locking it. "Do you want to get something to eat? I know I'm starved."

Loretta hesitated, "I think I should head home. I'm really tired."

Tony walked over to Loretta pulling her into his arms, "what is wrong? Did I say something?"

Loretta pulled away. "Tony let's be realistic here. After you are done doing this wonderful thing for Trisha, you will be going home where you should be. And I will be here doing what I do. What I'm trying to say is let's not make it hard for either of us to say good-by when the time comes."

Tony's heart sank knowing what Loretta was saying was true. Not only was he enjoying her company their conversations, but she was beautiful and he felt strongly attracted to her. "You are right, absolutely right." Tony took a step back from her.

Loretta smiled at Tony. "Please don't be offended. It is best if we try and keep it professional. I'll call you in a couple of days. In the mean time this is a list of papers I will need from you. Have them faxed to my number.

Tony took the folder from her hands and watched as she started her car and drove off.

MEMORIES OF LONG AGO

Loretta's legs were still trembling with excitement by the time she got home. Now she knew how her friend Connie had been swept totally off her feet so many years ago when it came to Tony. He was one desirable man, no doubt about it. The way he took her into his arms at the ranch, kissing her. She felt her body wanting more, to feel him inside of her. Did Connie tell her about their love making? She couldn't remember the conversation if she had. She was sure they had. They always talked about the men in their lives. Suddenly her heart ached. She missed her friend. Tears came to Loretta's eyes as she remembered years of being with Connie. Her own parents had taken Connie in and raised her after she had lost her parents. The holidays, the birthdays they shared. They were so close, like sisters. The memory came flooding back to the horrible night she lost her best friend. And now after all these years, Tony comes back into town. He meets Trisha and wants to buy back her home. Loretta sat on her sofa and grabbed a Kleenex to wipe her tears. "And I am in the middle of it," she said out loud. "Connie what would you say? Would you hate me for helping him? Would you hate me if I slept with the man?" She sat waiting, desperately hoping to hear Connie answer her. Nothing came but silence. After Connie's death, Trisha insisted she was seeing and talking to her mother. She was only around five years old at the time. Everyone thought it was just a little girl's way of dealing with her mother's death. Then one day something happened, something at the ranch. Rick wouldn't talk about it. Trisha would say. "He believes me now, he saw Mommy too." What ever happened that day, it changed Rick's life. He never drank after that. The cell phone she had put on her coffee table interrupted her thoughts. She looked at the caller ID. It was Tony. She hesitated and let it go to voice mail. She waited to hear the beep and listened to his message. "Loretta, I just want you to know how much I have enjoyed being with you. And I really appreciate all the work you are doing." There was a brief silence before he continued, "Good-night." Loretta climbed the stairs to her room, undressed and got into her bed.

THE DISCOVERY

Melanie pulled into the parking lot of the travel agency she worked for and shut off her car. In disbelief she watched as Becky exited the building and headed towards one of the three other vehicles in the lot. What the hell is she doing here? She waited for her to leave and then hurried into work.

Ann looked up from her desk and smiled. "Good morning sunshine."

"That woman that was just here, what did she want?"

"She just booked a honey moon package to Kauai.

"For who?" Melanie's eyes widened.

"She booked it for herself and her fiancé."

"Did she mention her fiancé's name?"

"Eric," Ann looked at the paperwork on her desk. "Yes, his name is Eric Maxwell. What is wrong, you don't look so good."

"That can't be possible. I know Eric he doesn't want anything to do with her."

Ann looked at her with sympathy. "Maybe he just wants you to think that. Some men can be very deceitful."

"No Ann, it's not like that. I have to call Eric and let him know what she is up to." Melanie took a step and then turned back to Ann. "How did she pay for this trip?"

Ann looked down at her paperwork. "She put it on Eric's debit card. She knew his pin number. She didn't spare any expense."

"Oh Ann, this is not going to be good." She sat down at her desk and pulled out her cell phone and dialed Eric's number.

"Eric," she said after he answered on the third ring. "I pulled into work this morning and saw Becky leaving. Ann says she booked a honeymoon package to Kauai for the both of you."

"What?" Eric said on the other end. "Tell me your joking Melanie."

"I'm not joking Eric. And she used your debit card."

"How the fuck, are you sure?"

Melanie walked over to Ann's desk and picked up the order sheet. "The card she used is a Visa and it has your name on it. You better call your bank and then you should call the police."

"Thanks Melanie, I will call you back."

Melanie set her phone on Ann's desk and sat in the chair. "He is going to look into this. I have to say Ann, this woman is scary. She really has to be off her rocker. She is the one that wanted to fight me that night you came to the gig. And I think she broke Eric's rear window the night he came over to my place. Now this, it is too weird."

"She's the one. I thought she looked familiar. Oh, honey I'm so sorry. You should have heard the way she talked." Ann shook her head, "it was like it was so real for her. She talked about her gown, how many people were coming to the wedding, and how the singer Tony Sands wrote a song just for them. And how her fiancé' Eric just wants her to be happy. I'm getting chills just thinking about it. You better be careful, if she thinks you are a threat there is no telling what she would do."

"I think your right. It might be a good idea if I stay at my brothers till we find out what is going on with her."

"Do you want to take a few days off? I want you to be safe."

"No, I don't think she would try anything with other people around. But thanks Ann. Can you fill Dale in on what is going on? He should know in case she comes around again. I still have to finish up the details for the couple from last week. But after that is it okay if I leave early? "

"Ann looked concerned. She stood up and walked over to the copy machine. "Sure, and give this to your friend Eric," she handed her a duplicate bill. "Maybe he can call his bank and put a stop on it before it goes through. I'll do what I can on this end. I'm sure the police will want it also."

Melanie quickly made her calls and reservations and smiled at Ann on her way out the door. She was working with an older woman and granddaughter on travel plans. Before getting into her car, she walked around making sure there were no flat tires. She then called Eric.

"Hi, is it okay if I come over. I have a copy of what she charged for the trip. You will probably want to give it to the police."

"God Melanie, you have no idea what this bitch did. I will tell you when you get here. It is a mess."

"I'll be there as soon as I can. Do you want me to get anything?"

"Yeah, can you get me a bottle of Jack Daniels? I need a drink. I called into work. I can't go in just now. I'm too pissed. Don't you have to work?"

"I asked Ann if I could leave early. She is concerned for us. She thinks I should not go back to my place for now, just in case Becky wants to come after me."

"That is not a bad idea. I don't want anything to happen to you Melanie. If anything happened to you I don't think I could forgive myself. I'm so sorry that you and your travel agency are involved in this."

"It is not your fault Eric. Becky is crazy, she needs some serious help."

"Or maybe she is sane and is just fucking playing games with us."

I'm at the store. I'll see you in a bit." Melanie hung up her cell and went inside and grabbed a cart. She picked up the bottle of Jack Daniels for Eric and a bottle of wine for herself. She also bought some chicken and potato salad for them. She wasn't sure if she could eat but maybe Eric would be hungry. Her mind was reeling and she felt nervous and concerned. She was concerned not only for herself, but for Eric. Hopefully the police would catch her and put her away before any more harm could be done. Until then she would have to watch her back. Maybe it wouldn't hurt to get a gun. She hated guns. She would think about it some more. For now she would pick up a small container of mace. She finished shopping and drove over to Eric's.

Melanie assumed Eric had just gotten out of the shower when he came to the door. He was wearing a pair of light faded blue jeans and putting on a shirt which he left unbuttoned, his hair still dripping wet. Melanie went straight to the kitchen and set the bag of groceries on the counter. She pulled out the box of chicken and potato salad. "Are you hungry? I thought you might need something to eat."

"Thanks so much for doing this. That does smell good." He stood next to her and pulled two plates down from the cabinet. Then went over to a nearby drawer and took out some silver ware.

Melanie took two glasses and filled them with ice and poured herself a glass of wine and started to pour the whiskey straight.

"No, I mix it with coke, I can't drink it straight. It will do a number on my stomach." He pulled a can out of the fridge and opened the top and poured some into the glass and filled the rest with whiskey.

They took turns putting food on their plates and then walked over to his kitchen table to sit. "So, give me an update." Melanie said taking a bite of her food.

Eric shook his head. "She is one fucking crazy bitch, man. I called my bank and found out she purchased a wedding ring set for over five thousand dollars and a wedding gown using my debit card. I had it set up so if my checking account went over it takes it from my savings so I don't get overdrafts. She depleted my savings, Melanie. Right now I am totally wiped out. I reported my debit as stolen and if it is within sixty days of me getting my statement I am not responsible for her purchases. It is going to take some time to get this bull shit straightened out and get my money back." Eric's phone rang, the caller ID telling him it was Shane. "Hey, can I call you back?"

"Have you been on our Facebook page? You are not getting married are you?"

Eric dropped his fork and quickly walked over to his desk computer and clicked on the bands page to see what Shane was talking about. "That fucking bitch," he yelled.

Melanie went to his side to see what was going on. There on the bands page she saw a photo of an engagement ring with an announcement that Eric was getting married to Becky. There were already a number of people writing congratulations and clicking the like button.

"God I can't believe this is happening." Eric said staring at the screen. Eric put his cell on speaker so Melanie could hear.

"Dude, you got to take that down, block her or something. Did you see what she wrote about Melanie?"

Eric scrolled the page down till he found what Shane was referring too. It was where Eric had written that Melanie was the new keyboard player in the band and included recent photos of her at the last gig. In the comment section Becky wrote Melanie was a slut and the only reason she got into the band was because she was screwing her fiancée.

"I'm going to kick her ass." Melanie said when she finished reading the comment.

Eric clicked the hide button and the removed her from the bands friends list. "Thanks Shane for letting me know. I've taken care of it."

"Hi Melanie, I think you should kick her ass." Shane said. "We need to keep her away from the gigs too."

"Let me call you back later. But you are right. I have to figure out how to handle this."

"Alright, if you need anything let me know." Shane said as he hung up from Eric.

"Oh no Eric, did you call the police? How could she use your card if it was in your name?"

"You bet I called the police. They put out a warrant on her. And I called the stores she went to. The bridal shop said they remembered her alright. They thought she was strange. But she knew the pin number. I have no idea how she got that. I was so pissed. I asked how the hell they could take a card that clearly had a man's name on it. Don't they ask for an ID? Both stores told me if I could get the items back from her and return them they would refund my money. I told them I don't want to go near the bitch. In the mean time, I immediately closed my account. The bank said they will keep an eye out for any suspicious transactions."

Melanie's cell phone rang and she went to her purse to grab it. "Hi Ann," she said. "I'm so glad to hear that. Thank you, I will tell him." She hit the disconnect button. "Well I have some good news. Ann was able to reverse the transaction on your card for the trip Becky purchased."

Eric rubbed his temples and sighed. "Please tell her thank you for me." Eric finished eating in silence and took his plate to the sink and rinsed it off. He then mixed himself another drink and sat down on his sofa.

Melanie did the same and sat down next to Eric. "Do you want me to leave?"

"No, please stay. I just don't know what to make of her. How did she get my card?" He pulled out his wallet and retrieved his debit card. He noticed the expiration date was coming up. "Shit," he said standing up abruptly and walking over to his desk. He pulled open a drawer. "That is it," he said turning to Melanie. "The bank sent out a new debit card. I distinctly put it in this drawer with my pin number attached to it. I was still using my old one because it wasn't expired yet. That means she has been inside my apartment. I have never brought her back here, Melanie. How did she find out where I lived? How the hell did she get in?" He walked over to the sliding glass door and opened it and looked at the lock. "I don't see any damage." He walked from room to room inspecting every window. He checked the front door also. He sat back down next to Melanie. "If she got in, I have no idea how she did it."

"Is it possible the manager or a neighbor let her in? Maybe she gave someone the same bull shit story she gave everyone else. Telling them she was your fiancée."

Eric picked up his phone and dialed a number. "I'm calling the apartment manager."

"Hello, this is Eric Maxwell from apartment one fifteen. I believe someone broke into my apartment. I was wondering if a woman might have come into the office saying she was my fiancée so she could get in. Kind of tall bleach blonde hair goes by the name of Becky."

"No, I'm sorry I don't recall anyone coming in the office asking to be let into your apartment. And if they did, we would certainly call the tenant first to get their permission. I suggest you call the police?"

"Yes, I already have. Thank you for your time."
Eric hung up his phone. "Well she didn't go to the office."

"Is it possible she had a key?" Melanie asked. "I know you wouldn't give her one. Are you missing an extra key?"

"I do, I have one I keep in a magnet box under my car. I will be right back," he said heading for the door. "Let me see if it is gone."

Melanie watched out the window as Eric walked over to his car and knelt down on the ground, feeling under the front driver's side. She then saw him stand up and walk back to the apartment.

"The key is still there." Eric said closing the door behind him.

"Is it possible she knew about the key and made a copy?"

"That is possible." Eric sat down next to Melanie and finished his drink. "This whole thing is giving me a headache. She has this insane idea that we are soul mates because we were both placed in foster care. My parents were drug dealers and the state came in and put me in foster care when I was young. The Richardson's were the last family I was placed with before I turned eighteen. Then I was no longer part of the system. Out of all the families I had been with, they were the best. They were an older couple with three children of their own. All of them grown. I would see them from time to time when they would visit. May was a stay at home mom and involved in the town and school activities. Carl Richardson was a music teacher for the local high school. Carl gave me my first guitar and taught me how to play. He showed me how to convert my anger and pain into something positive. He encouraged me to write my own songs. He also encouraged me to start my own band with other kids he taught. We called ourselves "The Wicked Knights," and practiced in the Richardson's basement. We eventually broke up and went our separate ways. It was also my time to move on since I was now past eighteen."

Melanie moved to the end of the sofa. "Lay down," she said placing a small blue couch pillow on her lap. "I'll rub your temples."

Eric laid his head down and closed his eyes as Melanie gently placed her hands on each side of his head and began the massage. "That feels good, thank you."

Melanie couldn't help noticing Eric's shirt was still unbuttoned revealing his tan hairy chest. Her excitement grew as she realized she wanted to touch more of him. She saw him looking up at her with an intense desirable gaze in his blue eyes. He raised his head to kiss her. She felt his soft lips touch hers, his tongue darting into hers. She ran her fingers along the hairs of his chest. He gently took her hand and guided it down below his belt. She could feel his erection and the excitement in her grew. He lifted her silky red shirt off and unhooked the front of her red bra letting her breast fall from the cups. He licked and sucked at each nipple as he fondled her. She moaned with pleasure. As she remained sitting on the couch, Eric kneeled on the floor. He removed her black skirt and red laced panties. He began licking her teasing her with his tongue. She moaned louder afraid she would come, wanting to and not wanting to. Eric stopped and pulled off his jeans and under ware. He took out a rubber from his wallet and put it on. He sat on the couch next to her as she climbed on top. No words needed to be spoken. She inserted his penis slowly into her. With each thrust going deeper inside, she felt an immense pleasure building. She gritted her teeth as she felt herself tightening around his penis not wanting to let go, not wanting it to end. Eric's thrust came faster and harder.

"Hold on baby, hold on." Eric whispered clutching her hips.

She dug her nails into the couch when the immense spasms of pleasure over took her, causing her whole body to shake from head to toe. Eric grunted as he thrust one more time. She felt his body relax beneath her. With a smile on his face, he opened his eyes and looked at her for a minute before kissing her.

"Well I guess I have something to thank Becky for."

"What?" Melanie said with confusion.

"You have to admit, if it weren't for her this probably would not have happened. I mean we both would have spent the day working, going home and doing what we usually do."

Melanie smiled and sat next to Eric slipping on her under ware and bra. "That is an interesting and positive way of looking at it. What do you think she will do when the police catch her? Do you think she will stay away? Ann said it sounded like Becky really believed everything she was saying. You hear this happening to famous people. You know where they believe they are having a relationship with the star."

"I am not a star. And if this is any indication of what a star goes through, I'm not sure I would want to be."

"Do you think anything like this has happened to Tony Sands?"

Eric shook his head. "I have no clue. She hasn't come into the club and started anything. I know Tony wouldn't like it if she did." Eric stood up and grabbed Melanie's hand pulling her to a standing position and kissed her. "I think I need some more consoling." She let him lead her into the bedroom. He gently laid her down on his bed and began to kiss her, taking his time until she begged him for more. He then mounted her and this time they started out slow until neither one could contain the excitement any longer, exploding into orgasms. She fell asleep in Eric's arms.

BECKY SEES DR. O'KEEFE

"Mom, Mom," she cried out, "noooo." It was the middle of the night when she was awoken by her own cries. Sweat dripped down from her forehead. She sat up in bed shaking. She was having another nightmare. She climbed out of bed and went into the bathroom and ran a washcloth under cold water and wiped her forehead and then held it over her closed eyes. She then returned to bed recalling the nightmare she has had since she was a little girl. There had been blood everywhere surrounding her mother as she saw her on the floor dead. She looked at the clock on her nightstand. She had four hours left before getting up for her appointment with Dr. O'keefe. She drifted off to sleep.

"It has been awhile," Dr. O'keefe said sitting behind her Mahogany desk. How have you been?"

Becky smiled as she sat and leaned back on the sofa. "I'm great, did you hear I am getting married?"

"I do believe your aunt mentioned it. I have to ask Becky, do you think you are ready for such a commitment?"

Becky ignored the question and leaned forward putting her left hand on Dr. O'keefe's desk. "See my engagement ring? Isn't it beautiful?" Becky asked smiling. "Eric told me to buy anything I wanted. Eric wants me to be happy. I have never been this happy before. We are so much in love."

"Is Eric aware of your psychological issues resulting from your childhood?"

Becky's mind faded out as she recalled that day. "It was pretty horrific. I was just a kid. No kid should have to see what I did. My Father did it. He would come home drunk and beat the shit out of her. She would tell me to hide in the closet and wait till she came and got me. But that day she didn't come to open the door. I was so terrified to come out. I must have sat there for hours. And when I did, I found her on the kitchen floor with a knife in her chest. I just wished I could have stopped him. I didn't even try. I could have called the police or ran to the neighbors when she started screaming. Maybe if I... " Becky went on, "I had to testify against my own father. You know he died in prison some years ago. I didn't go to his funeral. They said in court my mom was pregnant when she died. I hated him for what he did," she said bitterly. "I still hate him. I hope he rots in hell."

Dr. O'keefe spoke. "He was a horrible man Becky. But feeling hatred is not good for anyone. It can destroy your health and happiness you so much deserve. You were just a little girl. There was nothing you could have done to stop him that day. If you tried, he probably would have killed you too. He has already taken so much from you. It is time to let go of the past and move on."

Becky looked at her before speaking. "I don't know if I can."

"I think if you do, the nightmares will stop."

Tears formed in Becky's eyes as she reached for a Kleenex out of the box on the coffee table in front of her. "Even my adopted mother is gone. She was so good to me. Why is it everyone I truly love dies?"

"She died of cancer Becky. You told me yourself she suffered a long time with her illness. And again the illness was not your fault. You have no control over who gets cancer. There was nothing you could have done."

Becky lay back in the chair and closed her eyes and hoped the conversation was over for now. Her thoughts turned to Eric as she imagined herself climbing in bed next to him. She envisioned him cuddling close putting his arm around her waist as he kissed her, telling her everything would be alright.

Dr. O'keefe watched her client intently. Her mind going over what Becky just told her. Was this a breakthrough or was it the beginning of something else? "I'm afraid that is all the time we have for today," she said noting the clock on the wall. "Talk to my receptionist about another appointment. I would like to see you next week. I think you are making progress Becky."

BECKY GOES HOME

Becky drove up the long winding driveway that led to her home that she grew up in. She loved the house. It was a Victorian mansion with its spacious rooms. It had been in her family now for three generations. Part of the Sheldon Industries legacies. She could do without the old smelly furniture her aunt called antiques. To her it was junk. She parked her car by the garages and retrieved her suitcase from her trunk. As she entered the front door she could hear her aunt's voice barking orders at one of the staff. She then spotted her aunt wearing a decadent blue suit and watched her aunt smile slowly as she approached her. Her blonde hair neatly pinned up as always. She could see the taught flawless skin the results from her latest plastic surgery. Her aunt was seven years older than her father. She acted more like his mother then than his sister. She never married and lived with her adopted father in their mansion. After her adopted mother Carolyn died from cancer her father remarried but the marriage lasted six months and wife number two never returned. Becky thought her aunt was partly the problem as to why her father's second marriage never worked out. She would make their lives unbearable just like she did hers.

"Becky, how was your drive?" Her aunt gave her a kiss on the cheek. "You look exhausted. Let's go in the living room and you can sit and have some coffee and a sandwich." Becky put her suitcase down in the hallway and followed her aunt into the living room and sat down on the sofa. She slipped off her shoes and put her feet up on the couch and leaned back. "This feels good. Traffic was horrible. There was an accident and cars were backed up for miles until they could get it cleared."

"I really was hoping you could bring Eric with you this weekend. Give us a chance to meet him." Aunt Patricia looked down at her niece's hand. "That is a beautiful set you have. Isn't it customary to wait till after the wedding to wear the wedding band?"

Becky ignored the last question. "I told you Eric is very busy with his band. And he also runs Tony Sands night club. It just wasn't convenient to come along this trip." Becky looked away from her aunt. "So how is father? Will he be home or on one of his trips?" Becky was trying to change the subject.

"No, he will be home. He is looking forward to spending time with you."

Becky's cell phone began to ring. "Hello," she answered.

"Is this Becky Sheldon?" A deep voice on the other end asked.

"Yes, it is. Can I help you?"

"This is detective Reynolds from the Palm Springs Police department. We would like for you to come down to the station and answer some questions for us."

Becky quickly jumped off the sofa and excused herself and walked out of the room so her aunt could not hear the conversation. "What is this about?"

"We would like to talk to you about some purchases you made with a card that belongs to Eric Maxwell."

"I am out of town right now. Eric is my fiancé I'm sure he can answer all of your questions."

There was a brief pause. "You say he is your fiancé? Well I am sure he can but we still need to have you come in and talk with us."

"Then I'm afraid it will have to wait. My father is very ill and I'm sure you can understand how important it is that I stay with him. Have a good day detective Reynolds." Becky hung up her phone and turned her ringer off. She walked back into the living room sitting back down on the sofa.

"Was that Eric?" Her aunt asked walking in carrying a tray with sandwiches and 2 cups of coffee.

"Yes, he is so sweet. He was just making sure I arrived here safely." Becky heard the front door open and close. A few minutes later her father walked into the room. "Daddy," she jumped off the coach and ran into her father's arms giving him a kiss on his cheek.

"How is my little girl?" He asked returning her kiss. He was dressed in his business suit that he wore everyday to work. His tall thin frame towered over his daughter's. Her father was handsome just like his father before him. Tall, blonde hair and deep set blue eyes. The Sheldon family dated back to the early 1800's and they were proud of it. William's great, great Grandfather William Sheldon and his son William Jr. enlisted in the civil war at Lexington Kentucky together joining the Union side. On August 23rd 1862 both father and son served the battle at Big Hill, Kentucky. It is said it was the first sizeable engagement of the August 1862 Confederate Kentucky invasion. It pitted untrained cavalrymen against several of the more experienced Louisiana Confederate Cavalrymen with attached artillery. It was that day father and son deserted and later were caught and jailed. The father died in jail and the son was ordered to return to the war to serve out his enlistment. This story of their family was passed down generation to generation. Also adding it was a horrible war. Father William Sheldon Sr. had no idea what he was getting his son into until it was too late.

Aunt Patricia stood up. "I'll get you a cup of coffee and a sandwich."

Becky sat down on the sofa across from her father. Her phone began to vibrate in her purse. She noticed her father watching her.

"I'll get that later. I want you to have my undivided attention Daddy." Her aunt returned with another sandwich and coffee. She set it down on a table next to her father. She then returned to her chair.

"So what is this I hear that you are getting married?" Her father asked with a stern face. "Your aunt and I don't think you are ready for such a big commitment. You were ill for such a long time. You should give yourself a chance to adapt to being on your own for awhile. Does he know that you were institutionalized for a mental illness?"

Detective Reynolds turned to his computer and found more information on Becky Sheldon. She was the adopted daughter of Carolyn and William Sheldon who was a wealthy entrepreneurial. The daughter probably could have anything she wanted but chooses to do credit card fraud instead. She was probably just another spoiled brat trying to get Daddy's attention.   A few more clicks and he was able to find his home. This guy Eric must have scorned her and she was doing this for revenge. He had hoped she would come in and then he could arrest her. But that plan wasn't going to work so he would have to find her. He wrote down the address and grabbed his jacket and headed out the door.

HURT FEELINGS

When are you are coming back?" Eric asked concerned. "I mean now you are buying property out there. You have been gone a long time. Jen and I have been faxing over documents that you need to provide to some bank to buy a piece of property you say is for someone else. There is something you are not telling us. We just want to make sure you are okay. Danny came in and when I asked him about what was going on he said something about you finding out you have a daughter. This could be some sort of scam."

Tony laughed and knew it was Eric looking out for him. "I appreciate your concern. But this is not a scam."

"How can you be sure she is your daughter? Have you done a paternity test?"

"She looks just like me Eric. And it is more than that. I just know in my heart. No one is out to scam me here. In fact she would prefer I never contact her again. She has no idea I am doing this for her. It is going to be a surprise."

"Keep me updated on what is going on. Business is still booming here. The place is packed every night.

Jen has been busy digging out old photos and newspaper articles about the Quick shots from the basement and framing them to put on the walls. The customers really enjoy looking at them. A lot of them come in hoping to get a glimpse of someone famous. And the number one question is does the band ever get together here and play? If this keeps up Tony you might want to think about opening a chain of clubs."

"Tell Jen I said thank-you for doing that. I think it is a really good idea. And so is the chain of clubs. Maybe I will open a club here?"

"Maybe that isn't a good idea. You might never come home."

Tony laughed "one thing about Illinois, it gets mighty cold here in winter. I'll let you get back to work Eric. I'll probably come home after the closing which is scheduled to be in a couple of weeks."

"Tony there is something I think I need to tell you." Eric's voice became serious. "I've been having a problem with I guess you can call her a stalker. Anyways, she got into my apartment and got a hold of my debit card and pin number. She's a real nut case, Tony. She has it in her head I'm marrying her and she bought a wedding dress and a ring set. She tried to purchase a trip using my card where Melanie works at the travel agency. They were able to reverse the charge on that purchase but she wiped me out of my savings. She came to a gig and tried to go after Melanie. The police have a warrant out for her arrest but can't seem to find her. My concern is she might come into the club and start some trouble. I have told everyone at the club to be on the look-out in case she comes in. I just wanted to give you a heads up."

"Wow, over the years I've had women follow me but nothing to that extreme. Well I am glad you told me and keep me updated. Do you need any money? I can loan you some if you need it."

"Thanks Tony for the offer. I don't want to borrow from anyone if I can help it."

"Let me know if you change your mind. And thanks for getting the paper work for me and faxing it. I will give you a call next week." Tony hung up the phone and walked into the living room where Loretta was waiting. She had asked him to come over and go over some papers before the signing. He agreed only if she went to dinner with him afterwards. Every time they met, Tony kept his distance. As much as he wanted Loretta, he wanted this deal to go through more. He couldn't risk getting her upset and having her walk away. He might never see her again. Trisha might never get her home back. Each time they met, he would sit and try to concentrate on what she was saying. He had to push his thoughts, emotions, and desires for her away. Try to ignore his desire to hold her against his body. Try to ignore the sweet smell of her perfume. He wanted to feel the smoothness of her skin, her lips against his. And while trying to hide his erection from her sight. Even when he wasn't with her, his thoughts revolved around her. The way she smiled, the way she walked. He tried to convince himself he was lonely and home sick. He needed to get back to his club, his friends, his customers. He could have any woman, he was Tony Sands. But he knew she was different. She didn't want him maybe that was the attraction. The deal was almost done. He would be going home soon. The thought of leaving her made him sad.

"Tony, are you listening to me?" Loretta seemed annoyed. "I can't seem to keep your attention lately, is there something wrong?"

"Oh you have my attention alright. There is no problem there. Why do you have to be so beautiful? It would be so much easier if you were an old hag with missing teeth, or fat."

Loretta shook her head and smiled at him. "I will try and work on that for you. Until then, I believe you said you would take me to dinner." They both walked out to Tony's car that he was still renting and Tony drove to Heuer's Restaurant outside the town of Richmond. "It sounds like they have music tonight." They walked in and the hostess grabbed two menus. "Can we sit by the band? I'm sorry Loretta is that okay with you?"

"Sure, that is fine." She followed the hostess to a nearby table in the area where a four piece band was playing. There was a couple dancing to the slow melody that was familiar to her. She looked over at the menu and asked the waitress for a glass of red wine. Tony ordered the same. When the waitress returned with their drinks, she took their orders on the prime rib and walked back towards the kitchen.

"Do you care to dance?" Tony asked noticing her expression as she watched the couple on the dance floor.

"I would love too." She answered letting Tony take her hand to lead the way.

He held her in his arms as she followed his steps gracefully. As their bodies touched, Tony felt himself getting hard. He hoped the song would go on forever. How could she not notice the excitement that was growing inside of him, he thought. When the song ended, the tall skinny man on stage put down his guitar and walked towards Tony.

"Your Tony Sands aren't you?" The man asked with a smile holding out his hand.

Tony shook his hand, "yes I am."

The young man's smile broadened. "It would be an honor if you came up and did a song with us."

Tony looked at Loretta, "do you mind if I do a song with these guys?"

"Of course not, I would love to hear you sing."

Tony noticed a sparkle in Loretta's eyes and knew which song he wanted to sing for her. "Thank you," he said. He followed the guitar player and stepped onto the stage.

"We have a special guest that I am sure everyone will know." The room that was filled with people talking suddenly grew silent, as they turned to look on stage. "Please give a warm welcome to Tony Sands from the Quick Shots." The audience whistled and applauded. If they were not sure of who he was they recognized the name.

"Do you know 'The girl of my dreams?" Tony asked the band. It had been a huge seller for "The Quick Shots." Tony was not sure if they knew it. The song was released eighteen years ago. Tony thought these guys were probably still in diapers, when it first came out.

"We know it don't we guys?" The skinny guitar player said. "We know all your songs, Mr. Sands."

Tony smiled and listened as the drummer counted off one, two, three, four and the skinny guitar player broke into the melody of the song. Tony sang as he watched Loretta gracefully sitting in the soft candle lit table for two. Noticing how beautiful her green eyes were as she watched him and her soft silky red hair falling below her shoulders. He couldn't keep his eyes off her. The people in the audience turned to see who he was singing too. The song ended and people stood up applauding and whistling, yelling "one more, one more."

"Thank you, thank you." Tony spoke into the microphone. "Just one more" he said. I can't take this lovely girl out to dinner and expect her to starve most of the night. She might never go out with me again." The audience laughed and continued to applaud when they recognized the next song he started to sing.

After the song ended, Tony shook the hand of everyone on stage and thanked them for asking him to join in. The band continued playing music as he stepped off the stage and walked to the table where Loretta sat.

"That was wonderful." She said smiling. "Do you still play with the Quick Shots?"

"It is funny that you mention that. Eric, the guy that manages my club, says business is so good he thinks maybe I should open a chain of clubs. I was even thinking about asking for your help in maybe opening up one here in the area. Of course that means I would be spending a lot more time here, with you. I don't know if you could or would like that idea. What do you think?"

"I think that would be very, very exciting." Loretta reached out to touch Tony's hand and then pulled away as if unsure by the gesture.

"You do?" He asked taking her hand again. This was the first time she showed affection towards him besides the time he kissed her at the ranch. "What is it Loretta? Are you not attracted to me? Because I have to tell you Loretta, it is driving me crazy being around you."

"Tony it is a lot of things." Loretta took a sip of her wine before continuing. "Connie was my best friend. Trisha is like my niece and you are," she hesitated, "a musician. I know you probably have a lot of women in your life. I don't want the drama. I don't want to see a photo of me crying on the cover of some tabloid at the local check-out counter. Girlfriend Loretta finds Tony

Sands in bed with famous model. That is not the kind of life for me."

Tony sat back in his chair and looked at Loretta shaking his head trying to make sense of what she just said. He felt angry at her accusations. "You say I am a musician as if it is a dirty word. As if all musicians are whores or something. Is that what you think of me? First I will have you know, as far as me having a harem of women, all I can say is, I don't. I work my ass off at my recording studio during the day mixing sound helping other bands that are hoping to make it big someday, knowing they probably don't stand a chance. It's not that they don't have talent, it is just the competition is so tough. There are too many talented musicians out there. And then you watch the ones that loose whatever chance they might have at success because they get pulled down into the drugs and alcohol scene. Then I go to my club in the evenings to check up on how my business is doing before I go home tired and alone. I don't have young beautiful models like you think throwing themselves at my feet begging to sleep with me. As far as the press goes, they could care less who I see now. I'm old news. The only reason my name has been in the paper recently is because Ted died. After a month or so, no one will care who I am or what I am doing. And second, I don't see what this has to do with Trisha. And Connie is gone," he emphasized. "I think this loyalty towards your once upon a time friendship with her, is now pointless. I might be able to understand if she were still alive. I know unlike men, women have rules with their friends when it comes to this sort of thing. But come on, do you think she will come back from her grave and pick a fight with you? Is that what you are really afraid of? Or is it that you are afraid of taking another chance at love and happiness. I think it is easier for you to run away from your emotions?"

Loretta stood up from her chair so quickly it fell over. "Maybe it is because you are such an asshole. How dare you, I want to go home. You know what, don't bother, I'd rather call a cab." Loretta picked up her chair and quickly walked out of the restaurant.

Tony remained seated and tried to avoid the stares from other tables. Now he did it, he thought to himself. The evening was going so good and he spoiled it by getting upset at her and saying things he should of never of said. He waived to the waitress to come over and asked for the check. After giving her some cash and telling her to keep the change, he hurried outside hoping she was still there so he could apologize. But she was gone. He tried calling her phone but there was no answer. He got into his car and drove around to look for her to no avail. Reluctantly he decided to head back to the hotel feeling depressed.

SUNDOWN CREEK

Loretta sat in her office going over the final papers for Sundown Creek Ranch. The closing was in a few days. She had not talked to Tony since that evening she stormed out of the restaurant a week ago. He had left several messages urging her to call him, apologizing for the things he said. It was better this way, she told herself. She had to call him to let him know everything was set. They would all meet at Sundown Creek for the closing. And she was about to call Trisha and Rick with a story to get them out there. She dialed Trisha's phone number. It would take a lot on her part to make it sound like nothing out of the ordinary was going on.

Trisha answered on the third ring. "Hi Loretta, you must be really busy, I have not heard from you in a while."

"Yes, I have been. You have no idea. Sweetie, I hate to do this to you but Sundown Creek has been sold and the new owner says he has some questions and would like for you and your dad to come out Sunday afternoon."

"Yes, I noticed the sign when I drove by last week. It said sold. You can give the new owner dad's number. I am sure he won't mind."

"Well it is more than that. He says he found some things that probably belong to you. Thinks they might be valuable. I really think you and Rick and Sue should go. And afterwards I'll buy dinner. It's been a while since we went out. It will be like old times. I can't tell you how much I miss you and Rick," she pleaded. I guess you can say I'm kind of lonely." Loretta hoped she sounded convincing.

Trisha hesitated, "let me call my dad and see what he wants to do.

Loretta let out a sigh of relief. Now she had to call Tony.

It took a lot of work to convince Rick and Trisha they needed to check out what was left at the ranch but it worked. Sunday came and she was to meet everyone at the ranch. She got there early and found Tony walking out from the barn to greet her. She knew seeing him again would be difficult. Her legs began to tremble and her heart started to race. But she was determined not to let her emotions show.

"I can't wait until Trisha and Rick find out what you have done for them."

Tony smiled, "there is more, but let us go inside. I don't want them to pull up and see me standing out here."

Loretta followed Tony inside to the living room. A big banner hung over the fire place that said "Welcome Home." Blue and white balloons filled with helium were floating all around the room. A huge arrangement of roses stood in the corner near the fire place on the floor. "This is nice Tony," Loretta said looking around the room. "They will be so happy. How did you get in here?"

"I asked Carl for a copy of the key. I hope you don't mind. You weren't returning my calls."

"Oh," Loretta nodded understanding. "That is fine. I'm glad he was able to do that for you." She felt embarrassed now by her behavior realizing he had to go to Carl instead of her. "He should be here soon. The way it works is he will go over the paper work with Trisha and Rick and," Loretta heard a car pull up and looked out the window. "Carl is here." She said as she watched her boss park next to her car.

THE SURPRISE

"I really don't want to do this." Sue said sitting in the front seat next to Rick who was driving out of town towards Sundown Creek. "That was our home. It almost destroyed all of us when we had to leave. I don't understand why Loretta is putting us through this. I'm so glad we didn't bring the boys with us."

"I'm with you, honey." Rick patted his wife Sue's leg to comfort her. "We will quickly see what the new owner wants to show us and be on our way. Are you okay Trisha?" Rick looked in his rearview mirror at his daughter sitting in the back seat.

"Yes Dad, I am fine." She tried to sound convincing. She was mad, really mad at Loretta for putting her parents and herself through this. This was something she didn't think she could ever forgive Loretta for. It was hard enough to still live in the same area and have to drive by and see the home they had all loved so much. This was the place where her mother would go riding before she died. The place her father bought because it held so many memories of her mother. And the place that created new memories for her step mother Sue and her brothers. The fond memories she shared with her brothers, running through the meadows in the early evening. Catching fireflies seeing who could catch the most. They would hide in the hayloft playing hide and seek or make forts. She loved all the horses that they raised here. She remembered the night her own horse being born. There was a terrible storm, pouring rain and lightning streaked across the sky. She was about twelve when she remembered Sue telling her to put on her raincoat and grab her umbrella and follow her to the barn. Once inside the barn, Trisha saw Layla on the ground on her side sweating and squirming in pain. Trisha knew it was time for the colt to be born. Sue asked her if she would like to assist her with the birth.

"What do I do?" She remembered asking.

"I want you to sit down next to her head and pet her, console her. Just let her know she is not here alone. That everything is going to be okay. Do you think you can do that?"

It was her first time she saw a colt being born. She watched as the mother's contractions grew stronger her legs strained and her grunts grew with each push. Then the foal's front feet came out followed by the shoulders.

"Only aid the mare if she needs it," Sue explained. "If she does, pull gently on the front two legs. You don't want to cause tearing or harm to the foal."

Trisha remembered the foal coming out and Sue removing the mucous and checking the colt. Afterwards Sue turned to her and asked if she would like to have the colt, to keep it for her very own. She named her colt Lightning. From that day on she knew she wanted to be a veterinarian. She assisted with just about every birth after that and learned a lot from Sue before going off to college. The car turned down the gravel driveway that led to the ranch. Her Father parked next to Loretta's and each of them got out of the car and looked around. She saw tears begin to form in Sue's eyes and felt her anger rising at Loretta for putting her parent's through this.

"I can't go in there," Sue said wiping her eyes. "I will wait in the car."

"I'll go in Dad, stay with Sue." Before her father could say a word, Trisha turned and headed towards the front door where Loretta now stood smiling.

"Aren't they coming in?" Loretta asked. "Oh, they have to come in." She waived her arm towards them. "Don't you make me come and drag you in," Loretta yelled.

"Don't do this Loretta," Trisha growled. "Don't do this to them. I will never forgive you for this."

Loretta looked at Trisha giving her a warm smile as she put her arm around her shoulder and whispered into her ear, "Oh I think you will, trust me."

Trisha was confused and watched as her parents reluctantly walked towards them. Trisha followed Loretta into the house her parents behind her.

"Welcome home," Loretta said looking at all three of them.

"What, I don't understand." Trisha asked looking at the banner and the roses that stood in the corner next to Tony and Carl. "What are you doing here?"

"It belongs to you Trisha, and you Rick. I bought it back from the bank. Free and clear, no mortgage. All you have to do is sign some papers and the title will be in your names. No strings attached."

Trisha could hear Sue crying behind her as she stared at Tony. She swallowed hard holding back her own tears. "You've got to be kidding me. You bought our home back for me, for us?"

Tony nodded. "I know it could never make up for what I did to your mother and you. I can't take back those years, my mistakes. I only can tell you I wish I had done things differently and hope you believe me.

Trisha turned and saw her father crying as well. In a nearby window that faced the meadow something caught her eye. She quickly walked toward the window to get a better look. "Oh, my god," she yelled turning towards Tony with her eyes wide. "You didn't," is all she could get out of her mouth. She walked over to Tony with tears rolling down her face and hugged him. She could hardly speak. "Thank you," she whispered. She then ran out the back door.

Loretta looked out the window. "Is that Lightning? You got her horse back too?" Loretta watched Trisha as she embraced the horse that she had grown up with. "Now you have me crying."

Rick and Sue and Tony stood at the window and watched. Rick cleared his throat. "I'm sorry I don't even know who you are."

Loretta laughed. "This is Tony Sands."

A shocked look came over Rick's face. "I don't know if I should punch you or shake your hand."

"I prefer the hand shake," Tony said.

Rick extended his hand, "Thank you Mr. Sands. You have made my family happy again. I thank you from the bottom of my heart."

"Please, call me Tony. And I'm the one that should be thanking you. You took on the responsibility of raising Trisha even after her mother died. That must have been very hard on you. I must say you did a wonderful job. She is a fine young lady. You should be very proud of her. I can tell she loves you very much. She didn't even want you to know I contacted her for fear it would hurt you. She made it clear that you would always be her father.

Rick smiled and nodded. "I think there is room in her life for both of us." Rick turned to Sue, "you better call the boys and tell them to start packing, they are coming home."

Tony and Loretta

Tony walked over to Loretta as she stood by the fence watching Trisha ride Lightning. "Am I still an asshole?" He asked with a smile.

Loretta looked at Tony and smiled back. "You did a wonderful thing. And getting back Lightning, how did you find her?"

"Carl helped me. What could I do, you weren't returning my calls. It is a good thing this town is small and everyone knows everyone. I might not have been able to find the new owner. With their help we loaded Lightning in the trailer and brought her here early this morning. I don't know much about horses but I think she was very happy to be back here. As soon as we let her out into the pasture, she took off running. It was like she knew she was home."

"She knew alright, horses are very smart you know."

"Well now, I made the horse happy. I made Trisha and Rick and his family happy. What can I do to make you happy?"

"Well, why don't you come with us to dinner and then afterwards we can go back to my place and figure that out."

Tony took Loretta in his arms and kissed her lightly on the lips. "It sounds like something that will make me happy too."

THE ARREST

Detective Reynolds drove up the long driveway leading to William Sheldon's home. He parked behind a car that fit the description of Miss Sheldon's vehicle. He exited his car and walked up to the mahogany double doors and rang the bell. A short heavy set woman answered the door whom he believed to be a servant. He showed her his badge.

"Hello I am Detective Reynolds with the Palm Springs police department. I am looking for a Becky Sheldon."

A tall slender woman came to the door and shooed the shorter woman away. "Can I help you Detective?"

"I am looking for a Becky Sheldon, is she here Ma'am?"

"Well yes she is can I ask what this is about?"

"I have a warrant for her arrest." He pushed the door open, stepped inside and looked around noticing the home was quite large. "Can you show me where she is?"

"William," the woman called to another room. "Please come in here."

A tall man with graying hair entered the foyer. There was a strong resemblance to the woman with the confused and frightened look on her face.

"William," she sounded distraught. "This detective says he has an arrest warrant for Becky."

"She is my daughter." The man said roughly. "What is this about?"

"Sir she is being charged with credit card fraud. She has been making purchases using a card that belongs to Eric Maxwell."

"Well that is her fiancé. I'm sure this is just some sort of lovers spat. And we can get this all straightened out."

"Mr. Sheldon I presume? I can assure you Eric Maxwell is not your daughter's fiancé. He is very serious about pressing charges and has also put a restraining order on her to stay away from him. And until you can get this worked out, I am arresting your daughter."

"My daughter is seriously ill." Mr. Sheldon's voice grew louder. "She is under the care of Dr. O'keefe who is her psychiatrist. I will have her committed back into the hospital. That is where she needs to be, not locked up in some jail cell," he demanded.

"That is funny," Reynolds smirked. "When I talked to her earlier, she said you were the one that was ill. Hire a lawyer Mr. Sheldon. Now can you bring her to me or shall I come back with a search warrant?"

The old man's blue eyes glared at the detective. "Patricia, bring my daughter down. And then call my attorney."

THE FIGHT

"She's been arrested." Eric said as soon as he heard Melanie's voice say hello. "They have her locked up for now." He was working in his office going over the line up for the following month when Jen came to the door saying detective Reynolds was here to see him.

"Thank god," Melanie said breathing a sigh of relief.

But detective Reynolds said she will probably make bail tomorrow morning after the judge sets the amount. Apparently her pops is very rich. So I think it would be a good idea to stay at Nathan's for a few days longer."

"And where do you plan to stay? You're the one that has probably really pissed her off by now. She just might want to come after you with a vengeance."

"I can take care of myself. I plan on going to the bail hearing tomorrow to see what happens."

"I'm going with you." Melanie stated.

"I don't think that is such a good idea."

"If you are going, I am going. I want to see what happens to this bitch."

"She is a rich bitch." Eric replied.

"I don't care how rich she is. What she did to you is wrong. She wiped you out of your savings. She should pay for it with jail time. If she gets off with this, we should go to the press. I am sure daddy wouldn't want that to happen. If I were you I would be on the phone talking to the prosecutor making sure she does not get away with this."

"You are right. This whole thing could easily get swept under the rug. I will call him. Will you have dinner with me later?"

Melanie's voice calmed down. "Okay, can you pick me up at Nathans around six? I still have some client bookings I am working on. I probably will have to stay late to get those done. I will let Ann know I won't be in tomorrow or at least I will be late."

"Sounds good, I will see you then. Oh and Melanie, thanks for being here for me. It means a lot to me. Maybe after dinner we can go over some of the songs we started working on."

"That sounds good to me. Nathan has a piano at his place. He can get in on what we are working on. I'll see if he wants to go to dinner with us if that is alright with you?"

"That will be fine." Eric knew he wasn't exactly popular with the rest of the band, especially Nathan. He was hard on them that first day in the recording studio when Nathan brought Melanie in. He knew he had been a total asshole. Tony Sands had convinced him she would be good for the band. And he was right. Now he was realizing Melanie was also good for him. There was something in her that he felt changed him. He had always avoided relationships with woman. Up until Melanie his way of life would be to spot an attractive woman dancing and all he had to do is make eye contact and they would be his for the taking. He would approach them on break, buy them a drink and have sex with them after the show. Then the same pattern would follow. The girl would show up for the next gig and the gig after that. He would see her up on the dance floor wiggling her ass in front of him, as if saying I'm here take me. They seemed to want more from him than he could give, emotionally that is. Then there were the girls that would get up on stage with him to dance. That really annoyed him. Some nights there would be as many as three women sitting at various tables in the audience that he had sex with. On those nights he felt extremely uncomfortable. He would ignore them and avoid going to the bar on break. He'd ask either the drummer or the bass player to get him his drinks. He would remain with the rest of the band with his back turned toward the women he was ignoring. He could almost feel their eyes burning holes in his back. Chances were they would not approach him unless they were really drunk. If they did, he would cue the band break was now over and they would go back to the stage and start playing. This would aggravate the other band members, especially the drummer because he didn't have the time on break to piss. "Dude, you got to quit doing this to me man. I'm afraid I will end up needing a permanent catheter." He would have to wait until Eric did a guitar solo and then run to the washroom.

He spent most of the day in his office working on bookings and the staff schedules. At two o'clock he took his lunch break sitting at the bar ordering his regular sandwich from Jen. A couple of the regulars sat at the opposite side sipping their beers and watching the sports channel on the television that hung above the bar. Not too many customers this time of day. Later when the bands began to play the place would be packed. Jen brought him his food and a coke.

"Have you heard anything from Tony?"

"It sounds like things are going good for him. He closed on the ranch that he bought for the woman he believes to be his daughter and it sounds like he has something going on with this Loretta person that helped him with the deal."

"Did he say when he was coming back?"

Eric swallowed his food and took a drink from his glass. "He mentioned maybe opening another club like this one in Woodstock, Illinois. If he does I imagine he will be staying there longer."

"Where did he get such an idea? Are you sure these women aren't taking advantage of him?"

"I gave him the idea. I told him business has been so good since Ted died that he should open up a chain of clubs."

Jen gave Tony a smirked look. "So we have you to blame for this if he does not come back."

Eric finished his sandwich and downed his coke. "He'll come back. He hates cold weather." He stood up and pulled a few bills out of his wallet. Free lunches were included with being a manager. But he always left her and the bartenders a nice tip. "I will be late coming in tomorrow. The bail hearing for that psycho bitch Becky is in the morning."

Jen took away his plate and empty glass and wiped the bar down. "Good luck with that."

"Thanks," he said as he left the bar. He then drove home to shower and change before driving over to Nathans.

He arrived fifteen minutes early. Nathan opened the door. He had been here one other time to drop off some new songs that Nathan was learning when he first hired him for his band. Mostly he would see his band on gigs or at the studio.

Nathan closed the door behind Eric. "Melanie is still getting ready. Come on in and sit down. Would you like something to drink?"

"No I'm good, thanks." Eric took a seat on the sofa. I figured after we get something to eat we can come back here and go over some new material. Is that okay with you?"

"That is fine. I'm sorry to hear about your problem with that Becky chick." Nathan sat in the chair across from Eric. "Melanie was saying Becky had a key and got into your apartment. Wow dude that is pretty scary."

"And the thing is I never took her back to my place. So she had to of followed me home at some point. And I have no doubt she probably followed me to Melanie's the night my car window was broken. I feel better that Melanie is staying here with you until that bitch gets locked up. I have a restraining order against her but I don't know how crazy she is. We go to court tomorrow. And I go talk to the prosecutor to let him know I'm not taking this lightly. I want him to go after her and make sure she does not get away with this."

Melanie walked into the room. She was wearing tight faded blue jeans tucked into a pair of designer brown leather boots with heals. Her wavy brown hair shined as it cascaded around her shoulders. The shirt was the one she wore to their last gig. The top three buttons were left open revealing the curves on her suntan breasts. Her perfume she just applied lingered past Eric as she walked past him picking up her purse. "Let's go, I'm starving. Anyone have objections to going to Bills Pizza?"

They all drove in Nathan's car and walked into Bill's. The place was packed for a Wednesday night. They found a booth in a nearby corner and took a seat.

Melanie sat next to Eric with her brother across from them. They glanced at the menu and decided Pizza was it. Melanie ordered a glass of red wine and Eric and Nathan ordered two beers. The waitress wrote down on her pad and came back shortly with their drinks.

Eric noticed Nathan giving them both a peculiar look. "What's up man?"

Nathan leaned back against the booth smiling at Eric and then Melanie. "You," he stated with his eyes narrowing and his smile slowly fading. "You two got something going on." He tapped his fingers on the table as if he was trying to figure something out. "You're screwing my sister." Nathan blurted it out, shaking his head in denial. "No man, no, no, no. Please tell me I'm wrong. I know you man, you can't keep your dick in your pants for anyone."

"Jesus Nathan," Melanie yelled pounding the table with her hand. "Leave him alone. He has enough to deal with right now without you giving him shit."

The waitress came to the table and set down the pizza and plates. "Can you keep it down please?" She said in a low voice. "We have other customers here."

The three of them did not say a word as if scolded by their mother. They each took a slice of pizza and ate in silence. The waitress came and took the plates away.

"I will have another beer and a shot of whiskey," Eric said.

"I'll have the same," Nathan chimed in.

The waitress looked to Melanie. "No thanks, one of us has to drive." The waitress returned with the drinks and left. "I thought we were going to go over some new material. I can see that is not going to happen. Come on finish your drinks and let's get out of here. I'm not playing nurse maid for you two." They finished their drinks and paid the bill and walked outside. Melanie reached out with her hand open. "Give me your keys Nathan."

"I'm okay to drive." Nathan said with irritation in his voice.

"I said give me your keys." Melanie demanded.

"Don't be such a pussy," Eric said. "Just give her your keys so we can go home."

"Fuck you man," Nathan said as he raised his fist and swung hitting Eric square in the eye sending him to the ground. "And I want you to stay away from my sister. She deserves someone a lot better than you."

Melanie yelled at Nathan. "You don't choose who I see and who I don't see."

Eric got to his feet quickly and swung a punch at Nathan hitting him in the mouth. Melanie got in between them. "Stop this, stop both of you," she yelled. They could hear the sirens coming down the road. "Let's get out of here." Nathan gave Melanie his keys and got in the front seat and Eric got in the back. They drove past the squad car with the flashing lights that was headed to Bill's.

Nathan breathed a sigh of relief and reached into the glove box where he had some napkins and wiped the blood from his lip.

"You know, Nathan," Eric said from the back seat. "If you don't think I'm good enough, than I think you should find yourself another band."

"Knock it off you two," Melanie said clenching the wheel. "No one is quitting the band." She pulled into her brothers parking spot and turned off the car. She handed the keys to Nathan and got out of the car. Nathan got out also and then Eric. "I'll call you tomorrow," she said to Nathan.

"You are not staying here?" Nathan turned to her.

"No, I'm going to court tomorrow with Eric."

"Fine, whatever," he turned his back on Melanie and Eric and walked towards the front door.

Melanie turned to Eric with her hand held out. "Give me your keys."

Eric dug into his pocket and retrieved them and handed them to Melanie. "You don't have to do this you know. Maybe it would be best if you stay here tonight. He is pretty pissed."

"That is his problem. He will get over it. Let's go, I'm tired." They drove to Eric's and once inside, Melanie went to the refrigerator and grabbed ice cubes from the tray and wrapped them in a towel and handed it to Eric who had sat down on the sofa and turned on the television. "You need to put this on your eye. It is swollen and turning black and blue. I'm sorry for Nathan's behavior."

Eric took the towel and put it up to his eye and felt it sting. He got up and walked into the washroom and looked in the mirror. "Is he always so protective of you?"

Melanie followed him and leaned against the doorway with her arms crossed. "Sometimes, but he has never hit anyone I have dated before. You're the first."

"Lucky me," Eric smiled at her in the mirror.

Melanie raised her eyebrows and gave him a half smile and turned and walked across to the bedroom and undressed and climbed into bed. Eric put the towel in the sink and after undressing. Lay down next to Melanie, he reached over and ran his hand along her breast and then down her thigh as she moaned with pleasure. He kissed her neck and then her breast as he sucked on her nipples. He felt himself getting excited but waited until she begged for him to enter her. He held off coming until he felt she was ready and then their bodies melted into one in a wild frenzy. As he lay on top of her catching his breath he stroked her hair and kissed her sweet lips. He rolled off of her and held her in his arms as they both drifted off to sleep.

COURT

Eric and Melanie arrived at the court house early so he could speak to the prosecutor. Eric spotted him down the hall as he walked towards them with a brief case in his hand. "Mr. Lancing," Eric reached out to shake his hand. "I am Eric Maxwell, the one that Becky Sheldon ripped off. I want you to make sure she does not get away with this. What she did was commit fraud and she wiped me out of my savings." Mr. Lancing was a tall man in his mid fifties with graying hair. Judging by the way he was dressed in a slick black suit, Eric figured he made good money being a prosecutor.

"How did you get the black eye?"

"Her brother it is a long story."

"Let's go over here and sit down." He walked to a bench and opened his briefcase and looked over some papers. "I see she used your debit card to make some purchases."

"She stole my debit card and went on a spending spree. I have no money left. I had my account set up for overdraft privileges. And when she depleted my checking account it withdrew from my savings."

Mr. Lancing looked at a piece of paper and then over at Melanie and then Eric. "She is saying you are her finance'."

"No, no, no." Eric shook his head. I was never engaged to her."

Melanie came closer. "She is crazy, she even came into where I work at the travel agency and tried to book a honeymoon telling my boss she was marrying Eric. We were able to reverse the charge before it went through."

"And you are?" Mr. Lancing asked.

"My name is Melanie, I'm in his band. And no, this is not some kind of lover's spat between them. She is nuts, and dangerous. She's gone after me and broken his car window. God knows what she is capable of doing."

Mr. Lancing put away his papers and stood up. "Today the judge is just setting the bail amount and a future court date to deal with her charges. By what you told me, I can let the judge know that she could be a danger to both of you. We can only hope he will set the bail amount high. But her father is a wealthy man and I'm sure raising the amount won't pose a problem for her."

Melanie and Eric looked at each other with concern. They followed Lancing into the court room and took a seat two rows behind him. There were four other cases called before they brought Becky in from a door off to the side. She was seated at a nearby table up front next to a well dressed older balding man, Eric presumed was her lawyer. She was dressed in a black pants outfit that she wore when she was arrested. She looked around the room and smiled and waved at Eric. Her smile turned to scorn when she looked at Melanie. "Maxwell versus Sheldon," the bailiff said loudly. The prosecutor approached the bench as did Becky's lawyer. Melanie and Eric could not hear what was being discussed with the judge. The discussion ended quickly and both lawyers returned to their tables.

"Miss Rebecca Sheldon," the judge looked at her gravely. I am extending the restraining order Eric Maxwell has placed against you. You are not to go within five hundred yards of where he is. This includes emails, phone calls anything that puts you in touch with Mr. Maxwell. If you do, you will be arrested. Do you understand Miss Sheldon?"

The man in the suit leaned over and said something to Becky. "Yes I do," Becky said in a soft voice.

"Court date will be set for February twenty second bail is set for fifty thousand." The judge pounded his gavel and the bailiff called the next case.

Eric and Melanie watched as an older man went up to Becky and hugged her. She turned towards Eric and Melanie and showed no emotion this time. She was escorted away by the officer.

The prosecutor came up to them. "Let us go outside."

They followed him out of the courtroom. "Her lawyer is paying the bail as we speak. From there she will be released. The best I could do was to ask the judge to extend the restraining order. As you heard she is not allowed within five hundred yards of you. I can tell you I think her lawyer will be using the defense that she is mentally impaired. That she has a Delusional disorder and is not aware of what she is doing."

"What," Eric said out loud. "You got to be kidding me."

"Is it true? Is she mentally ill?" Melanie asked with alarm.

"I don't know I do know they will have to prove it in court. I have to prepare for my next case. Can I have your phone number Eric? And here is my card."

Eric took the card and placed it in his wallet and pulled out one to give to the prosecutor. It was one he carried to give out to clubs in case they were interested in hiring his band. "My home and work number are on there. Thanks for what you did, but I'm concerned about Melanie's safety as well. Can we include her in the restraint order?"

"The judge will require documentation of harassment in the form of a police report before the order will be made official. Has Miss Sheldon threatened you?" Mr. Lancing asked Melanie.

"The first night I played out with the band. She was there and she tried to throw a punch at me."

"Were the police called, did you make out a report?"

"No," Eric replied. "I took her outside and told her to leave."

"Well I'm afraid at this point the judge would deny Melanie a restraining order from Miss Sheldon. I really must go now. My office will keep in touch."

Eric and Melanie watched as Mr. Lancing hurried down the hall. "Come on," Eric said. "Let's get a bite to eat." Eric drove to his favorite diner where he ran into Melanie after she first joined his band. They took a seat in a nearby booth and the waitress brought the menus.

"I will have the egg omelet special and coffee please." Melanie said handing the waitress back the menu.

"Make that two." Eric said. He looked out the window remembering the last time he was here seeing Melanie walk in and then joining him. He turned to her, "I'm sorry I was such a jerk that day I ran into you here."

"Apology accepted," Melanie smiled. "When we leave here, can we stop off at my brothers and get my things. I would like to pick them up before he comes home from work. I'm not staying with him, I'm too pissed."

"You are not planning on staying at your place? It can be dangerous, Becky knows where you live."

"And she knows where you live too."

Eric thought for a second and took out his phone. "I've got an idea." He dialed Tony's number. The waitress brought their omelets and set the plates down. "Hey Tony," Eric said into the phone. "How are things going?"

"Great," Tony replied. "I think Loretta found the perfect place for my new club. It needs some work. It has been abandoned for a few years. But it has potential. I'll send you photos. How are things there?"

"The club is doing great. But I'm having some issues with that stalker I was telling you about. It seems she has a delusional disorder, or at least that is what her lawyer claims. Anyways the prosecutor was able to extend my order of protection from her but it does not cover my friend Melanie. The psycho bitch Becky knows where we both live. I was wondering if it would be okay if we stayed at your place?"

"Sure, I guess that would be okay. I have an extra key in my office in the middle draw. My alarm is on so you will need the code number to get in. Otherwise the alarm will go off and the cops will come. The number is six, two, four, and six."

Eric wrote it down on a napkin and put it in his wallet. "Thanks Tony, I can't tell you how much this means to me. How did things go with your daughter and you buying her the ranch?"

"She is thrilled to be able to move back home. I even managed to get her horse back. It was really emotional for everyone. It made me feel so good to be able to make them happy. I've been given a second chance

Eric. Take my advice and don't ever deny yourself some time to love like I did for so long. There is no greater gift you can give and receive."

Eric looked up at Melanie as he thought of what Tony just said. "I think that sounds pretty wise."

"Keep me updated, and be careful."

"I will," Eric said. "And thanks again."

FAMILY

"What was that all about?"   Loretta asked as she kissed Tony.

He put his arms around her and held her tight. "Have I told you that I love you?"

Loretta laughed, "only about a million times.   But don't ever stop telling me. I love you too I hope you know. Now come on, Trisha has dinner on the table."

Tony and Loretta walked from the car into the house. There was no need to knock, his daughter expected him home for dinner just about every night.   Trisha was finishing putting the roast on the table.   Rick and Sue and the two boys were already seated and talking about the day's events. Tony and Loretta took their seats and joined in the conversation. They waited for Trisha to sit down. It was their ritual each evening to go around the table and say what they were grateful for that day before eating.

Tony paused and reached for Loretta's hand and squeezed her gently. He looked at Rick. "In the past few months I have worked side by side with you getting the ranch back to the way it was before the bank took it away. You are a good man Rick. I have enormous respect for you and consider you my brother. I am truly grateful for being included as part of this family. My life has truly changed for the best. I just got off the phone with Eric. I told him don't ever deny yourself some time to love like I did for so many years."

THE DEAL

Melanie walked around her brother's apartment picking up her items and putting them into a suitcase she had open on the chair. She looked around the living room and then sat down with a pen and paper in hand. She wrote,

Nathan,

I decided after last night. It would be best if I did not stay with you at this time. I want you to know I am still very angry with the way you treated Eric and I will call you in a couple of days.

Love Melanie

She left the note on the kitchen table and put the salt shaker on top to hold it in place. She zipped up her suitcase and both she and Eric walked out of the apartment, locking the door behind them. From there they drove to Eric's place so he could pick up some items for the stay at Tony's. The next stop was the club to pick up the house key. The club was closed every Monday.

"I am glad no one will be here to ask about my black eye." Eric said looking around at the empty parking lot. Melanie followed him in and he went straight to Tony's office and got the key out of the desk. He walked around the club checking to make sure everything was okay and set the alarm before locking the back door behind them. Once out of town Eric pulled onto a narrow road leading into the mountains. He drove another ten minutes and turned right, pulling into a circular driveway in front of a large off white stucco ranch home with brown shingles surrounded by palm trees and the view of the mountains behind it.

"Wow," Melanie said getting out of Eric's car as she looked at the home of where they would be staying. "Tony's home is beautiful."

"Wait till you see the inside. And there is a pool in the back." Eric grabbed the suitcases from the trunk and walked up the paved sidewalk that was lined with colorful flowers planted among the palm trees. When he unlocked and opened the front door he heard the beeps of the alarm. He punched in the code and the beeps went silent. He wheeled the two suitcases inside behind him and Melanie followed. The hallway walls were white and held three abstract paintings. The floor was off white marble leading to a large living room with a beige colored area rug that matched the sofa and chairs that sat in front of a modern stone fireplace. A flat screen television hung above the fireplace. Off to the side of the living room was a bar and stools. Behind it was a wall of glass windows from ceiling to floor showing a pool and in the corner a layer of three cultured stone steps leading to a hot tub surrounded by palm trees and lighting in the ground to accent them.

Deep green grass outlined the cultured stone patio that held an array of colorful purple Salvia flowers mixed with lighter colors of Salvia. A six foot privacy fence surrounded the pool area. Behind the fence and through the palm trees you could see the purple in the San Jacinto Mountains and the blue sky behind them. Eric led Melanie past the bar to the doors leading to the outside patio. From there one could see the roof of the house extending over a portion of the patio covering a built in fireplace and a small outdoor kitchen to cook in. The extended roof was made to look like a ceiling with a lighted fan and beneath it was a beautiful glass dining table that could easily seat six. The chairs had thick beige cushions. In the upper corner of the patio were speakers for music.

Melanie watched as Eric turned on the hot tub. "I am so going to be spending my time in there." She turned around taking in the view. "This is so beautiful. Tony must be very happy living here."

Eric walked up to her and put his lips on hers. "I think you are beautiful." He watched as a smile came to her face. "Come on I will show you the rest of the house." Eric took Melanie's hand and led her back inside down another hallway with several doors. They walked into a large bedroom with a fireplace and a walk out door that faced the pool area. There was a large bathroom with brown ceramic tiles for the shower and also a sunken in bathtub. Wall to wall mirrors above a long vanity also done in ceramic tile. "This is Tony's room."

"He must have a cleaning lady. His home is very clean and tidy for a bachelor."

Eric led Melanie to another bedroom down the hall. "We will be sleeping in here." The guest bedroom was only slightly smaller but not by much. It also had a television and fireplace and a bathroom. Eric gently pushed Melanie down on the bed and began to kiss her. She moaned as her hands grasped his zipper and her warm hands reached inside his jeans. Eric's excitement grew as he felt her hand squeeze his erection. He stood up to pull his jeans and shirt off. Melanie pulled back the quilted cover on the bed revealing red satin sheets and pillow cases. She ran her hand across the sheets and then turned her attention back to Eric who stood before her totally naked. He watched as she took his penis in both hands and began to lick him and then taking him into her mouth. He held back her soft hair with his hands as she brought him near to orgasm. He threw back his head and gently pushed her away. He was so close to coming but needed to be inside her. He quickly helped remove her clothes. As he lay down besides her, he began kissing her lips, her neck and down between her legs. She arched her back eager to feel his warm tongue as she moaned. When her moans became louder he climbed on top and entered her quickening his thrusts until both of them climaxed.

The phone that was inside Eric's jeans pocket that laid on the floor began to ring. Eric rolled off Melanie and reached down and looked at the caller ID. It was Mr. Lancing the prosecutor. Eric answered it. "Hello," he said.

"Eric, I have some good news. Mr. Sheldon called me and is willing to pay you back for the bills his daughter accrued and little more for the aggravation this has caused you, even though you are not liable for the amount. But in exchange he has asked that the charges be dropped. Mr. Sheldon informed me that his daughter had stopped seeing Dr. O'keefe and had stopped her medication. And by doing so, this brought the delusional disorder to return. I told him I would discuss this with you and get back to him this afternoon. Now what I would like to suggest is that you agree to the deal but include she must be committed to a psychiatric ward for evaluation and seek psychiatric help. If you don't agree she probably will serve some jail. Would you like to think about it and get back to me?"

Eric was silent for a moment as he sat on the edge of the bed thinking. "No, I will go along with what you think is best."

"Very well, I take it these are the total charges. I will give this to Mr. Sheldon and go over what we discussed. I will be in touch with you later this week when it is settled. Enjoy your day Eric."

"Thank you Mr. Lancing, thank you." Eric hung up his phone and turned to Melanie smiling. "Well it looks like Becky's Dad is going to reimburse me for the damage she has caused. And in return the charges will be dropped with the condition she be committed and seek psychiatric help. This is such a relief." Eric ran his hands through his hair and leaned back against Melanie's legs. I'm still going to have the stores reimburse me for her purchases. Those sales people should be fired for not asking for an ID and for believing her bullshit."

"That is good news. But just to play it safe, I think we should stay here for a week." Melanie smiled. "At least until we know for sure she is locked up."

Eric leaned over and kissed her on the lips. "I think that is a wise idea. Come on," Eric slapped her lightly on the butt. "Let's go up to Tahquitz Canyon."

BECKY RUNS OFF

The drive home from the courthouse with her father was quiet. She knew he was displeased once again with her. Her memory was vague as to why she spent the night in jail. And the judge ordering her to stay away from Eric, well she knew that was her father's doing. He would soon realize nothing would keep them apart. And if her father continued to try she would have no choice but to cut her father out of her life. He will have to learn to accept Eric as his future son in law. The car pulled up in front of their home. Becky was greeted at the door by her aunt who gave her a stern look as she walked past her and towards the stairs.

"Becky," her father said in a loud voice. "You are to pack your bags. You are going back to the hospital."

Becky stopped on the third stair and turned to her father. "Why do you hate Eric so much?" She watched as her father and aunt exchanged looks of disbelief.

"Please," her father said his voice starting to crack. "Just go and pack your bags."

Becky turned and ran up the stairs slamming her bedroom door behind her.

William Sheldon Sr. walked into the living room and over to the small glass table on wheels that held the variety bottles of Vodka, Brandy, and Gin. He poured himself a glass and downed it quickly. He turned to his sister who followed him into the room and waited till she sat down on the sofa. "She is sick, she spends the night in jail and the judge ordered that she stay away from this man and she still thinks there is some kind of relationship between them. She just does not get it. I talked to the prosecutor in hopes that we can get the charges dropped if I agree to pay for the damages she has caused. But I can't handle her anymore. She is out of control without her medication and when she is not seeing Dr. O'keefe." He poured himself another drink and sat down in his chair across from his sister, his voice softening. "Remember when she was a little girl we would laugh at her stories?"

Patricia smiled at her brother. "Yes, until her stories became a problem. I can't count how many times I would be called by her teachers and after hearing her story I would take her side and reprimand the teacher for the poor job she was doing. At some point I realized it can't be all of these teachers and her little friends. Oh how I wanted to believe her. I wanted to believe the problems were caused by someone else. I thought that maybe they were all jealous because her Daddy was rich."

"Carolyn wanted a child so badly. She felt it was her fault we couldn't have any of our own. I thought adopting Becky would change everything for us. And then when we heard what she had been through, her own father killing her mother. How could we not try and help a poor innocent child like that. But then the following year we found out Carolyn was dying of cancer. Maybe if Carolyn had not died, it might have changed things for Becky."

"I don't think Carolyn dying of cancer had anything to do with her delusional disorder. You can't blame yourself or me for the way she has turned out William. It is what it is. We have always been there for her."

Becky packed her suitcase like her father told her to. But she was not going back to the hospital. She would stay at Eric's. She quietly walked down the stairs, stopping to hear her father and aunt talking in the living room. She then quickly ran to the front door and went to her car that was parked on the side. Once she started her car she quickly put it in gear and drove off before anyone could see or hear her leave. She pulled onto the main highway headed through town. She stopped at the red light when she noticed Eric's car turning left in front of her. Becky recognized the woman who was sitting in the passenger seat. It was that Melanie chick. Anger started to rise from within her. She turned down the same road and left a few car lengths between them so as not to be noticed. She followed them out of town towards Tahquitz Canyon. She parked her car along the road and waited until they got out of the car and watched as they walked hand in hand down the trail leading through the canyon. Becky quickly followed them making sure she stayed close to the boulders so she could easily hide in case one of them stopped to turn around. She could hear their voices as they talked but could not hear the conversation. Occasionally she could hear Melanie giggle and that infuriated her. That should be her walking beside Eric enjoying the feel of his hand in hers, laughing at his jokes. She continued to follow them up the mountain through the Canyon. They had stopped a few times to take a break and drink from their bottles. Becky made sure she stayed hidden wishing she herself had something to drink. Then she watched as they continued their walk up the trail. They must be near the waterfall, she thought. She could hear it and see the water flowing from a nearby creek. The closer they got, the louder the sound of the water fall became. The trail was thin and led to some flat rocks that were laid in the water so you could step on them to cross in front of the waterfall. To follow any closer she would surely be seen. From here she would have to wait behind a boulder.

TRAGEDY AT TAHQUITZ CANYON

Eric watched as Melanie removed her shoes so she could step on the wet rocks that lay in the shallow stream that flowed from the sixty foot waterfall. She then reached for his hand to help guide her. Together they waded into the water inching their way closer to the waterfall. The day was hot and the cool refreshing water felt good on their bodies. Eric and Melanie swam behind the waterfall where no one could see them if they came by. He took her in his arms and kissed her gently. "I love you Melanie." He watched as her eyes sparkled and a smile came across her beautiful face.

"I love you too," she said.

Eric kissed her again holding her tight. He never wanted to let her go. He felt himself getting hard. He reached down and unzipped Melanie's shorts and helped her out of them. Then she unzipped his. He felt his way inside her, as she welcomed him with her moans. He wanted to stay inside her forever. To always feel her warmth, the wetness of her body, to be able to feel her tightening around his penis as he made love to her. Their warm bodies melting into one as the water from the Tahquitz fall splashed upon them. Both shivered with excitement as they came together.

"Let's go find a place where we can dry off." Melanie said handing Eric his shorts. They went back into the water and swam to the shore and climbed out. Melanie turned to the water fall. "This place will always hold a beautiful memory of this day for me."

Eric smiled, "me too." He took her hand and helped her up to the trail that would take them back through the canyon. They were high up into the mountains and it was a long way down. They walked up to a clearing that showed the canyon below. Eric stopped and looked at the mountains surrounding them in awe of the beauty of nature's tapestry that encumbered them. He watched as the sun canvassed light over the colored gray and magenta mountains that rose from the earth to the sky. Creating shadows deep in the crevices. He threw his arms in the air and yelled at the top of his voice. "I am in love with this woman." A hawk squealed as it flew off from a nearby tree as his words echoed through the canyon.

Melanie started to laugh when suddenly she was thrown to the ground from behind.

Eric turned around and saw Becky on top of Melanie hitting her as she tried to defend herself.

"You fucking bitch," Becky screamed. Her dark eyes wild, her face showing the depth of her hatred and anger. "Eric loves me, not you."

Eric ran to Melanie grabbing Becky at the waist pulling her off of her. But Becky grabbed a rock from nearby and turned and hit Eric in the head. Blood began trickle from his wound. She turned her attention back to Melanie who was now standing up. Melanie kicked Becky in the stomach causing her to double over. Recovering from the pain, Becky quickly stood up and continued towards Melanie waving her arm with the rock screaming "you are going to die bitch."

"Put the rock down." Eric turned to see a ranger with his gun drawn walking quickly towards them. "Put the rock down and step away from the edge lady."

Eric watched as Becky turned away from Melanie to see the ranger holding the gun towards her. Her face contorted with what Eric would later describe as pure evil. She turned back towards Melanie raising the rock over her head and lunged forward. Melanie quickly stepped aside and Becky went over the side of the mountain screaming as she went down, her head and body smashing into the jagged rocks below.

Melanie ran into Eric's arms shaking. "We need to get you to the hospital."

Eric held his hand up to the side of his head. "I don't believe what just happened. Are you okay?"

"I'm fine, just shaken that's all."

The ranger, who was about forty, was tall and wore a tan uniform, looked to be Native American. The ranger walked to the edge and looked down to see a woman's twisted body lying in a pool of blood. He turned to face Melanie and Eric. "There is no way anyone could have survived that fall. I saw what happened but I want a report from you both as to what went on."

"Can we get him to a hospital first? He is losing blood."

The ranger took out his cell and called down to the station. "I'm going to need a helicopter up here near the falls. Someone has been hurt. And I also have a DOA that went over the edge. He walked over to Eric and Melanie and used the recorder on his phone. "While we wait, can I have your names and tell me what happened with that young lady that went over the cliff."

Eric was sitting on the ground leaning against a boulder holding his head with Melanie beside him. His head hurt really bad, he let Melanie tell the ranger their names and how he had a restraining order against Becky. Twenty minutes later the sound of a helicopter was heard from above. They dropped down a stretcher and the ranger secured Eric in.

"Don't leave me," Eric said holding onto Melanie's hand.

"Sorry bud," the ranger said. "She can't go with in the helicopter. They will take you to the hospital and come back for the body. It is not easy for the rescue team to get into these mountains. It is going to be tricky to get the body out of here because of where she fell. Your girlfriend here will have to find another way to the hospital."

"Take my keys," Eric said. They are in my pocket." Melanie reached in and retrieved his keys. "I will be there as soon as I can get down off this mountain."

The ranger waved an all clear to the pilot. And Melanie wiped away her tears as she watched them hoist Eric into the air.

AT THE HOSPITAL

"You have a concussion and will need to take it easy for awhile," the doctor said. "I put twelve stitches in you." The doctor took out a pen light and checked his eyes.

Melanie came back into the room with a fresh cup of coffee and waited for the doctor to finish. She had stayed by his side for the first twenty four hours.

"You need to go home and get some rest. You look exhausted."

Tony and Loretta walked into the room. "If you wanted me to come home all you had to do is ask. You didn't have to go and get your head bashed in," Tony teased. He walked into the small hospital room that had two beds. He handed Eric a vase of flowers. Loretta followed behind him.

"Thank you," he smiled up at Tony. "Next time I will keep that in mind."

"Eric, this is Loretta my fiancée." Tony put his arm around her.

"Wow you are full of surprises. First you find your daughter and now a fiancée. It is nice to meet you Loretta."

"I'm Melanie," she stood up from the chair in the corner and shook Loretta's hand.

"So is there anything new on the chick that died?"

"We have been cleared of any wrong doing in her situation. The ranger saw what happened. It is a good thing too, or we could be facing murder charges.

The prosecutor said her father is deeply distraught by his daughter's death but is still willing to pay me back for all the debt she ran up on my card. So that makes me happy. That was so freaky Tony, I had no idea she was a sick bitch."

Melanie smiled and bent down and kissed Eric on the lips. Her phone from her purse began to buzz she reached inside and looked at the caller ID. She looked at Eric, "it is Nathan."

"You better go talk to him." He watched as she walked out into the hallway with her phone.

"Nathan is her brother," Eric told Loretta. "He does not like me. He said I'm not good enough for her."

"And he is still playing bass for you?" Tony laughed. "Find yourself another bass player."

"With all this shit going down with the psycho bitch and running your club, I have not had time to think about the band."

"Well I'm back now and you can relax, take care of yourself for now. That is what is important."

Melanie returned smiling. "Nathan would like to come up and see you. He says he wants to apologize and he feels really sorry for what he said."

"Okay kid, make up with your bass player. I'm going to take this lady home. If you need anything I'm here for you."

"Thanks Tony." Eric watched as Tony and Loretta left the room hand in hand. He was happy for his friend who had finally found love after all these years. Eric smiled remembering what Tony had said and mumbled the words. He felt the pain medication starting to take affect and felt really tired and trying to keep his eyes open.

Melanie turned to Eric and leaned in closer. "What did you say?"

"Don't ever deny yourself some time to love. That is what he told me." Eric drifted off to sleep with Melanie by his side.

ABOUT THE AUTHOR

I was raised in Algonquin Illinois. I have been around musicians my whole life and tend to write novels about this kind of life style.

I also sing with my husband Anton who is very talented and fills me with inspiration, humor and love.

I hope you enjoy my novels and you can find me on Facebook.